T0148604

Train Flight

Furry Friends

ELIZABETH NEWTON

ISBN: 978-1-4669-5603-2 (sc)
ISBN: 978-1-4669-5604-9 (e)

Trafford rev. 01/04/2013

 www.trafford.com

North America & international
toll-free: 1 888 232 4444 (USA & Canada)
phone: 250 383 6864 ♦ fax: 812 355 4082

Note:

This story is the forth of the Train Flight series. It can be read by itself, but it is also part of the ongoing adventures of Evie and Paulo in the Train with the Captain.

Others in the series so far:

Moon Man
The Birth Of Salvation
The Sanctuary

Contents

Chapter One

Show and Tell

The pale little girl waited eagerly for her turn. She wriggled and fidgeted on the floor, hardly listening at all to what was being said up front. Frustration and restlessness tore at her gut and her impatience boiled as she realised that a talking superhero action figure with movable arms really wasn't that interesting. It was a mercy only three comments or questions were allowed, only one comment was particularly and excruciatingly long due to the shy stutter of the commenter. But finally, the wonderful moment came when the speaker said, "Thankyou for listening," and the class replied "Thankyou for sharing," and Miss Reynolds said those magical words:

"Okay, Ruby, you're next. Up you come."

Ruby jumped up with a smile from ear to ear, ran to her desk and grabbed the ice-cream container she'd poked holes in the top of, and carried it over to stand in front of the class. She smiled at the class and licked her lips as if she was about to devour a large plate of ice-cream cake. She waited, purposefully building up the suspense for them. But to her dismay it only made them restless and some began to whisper amongst themselves.

"Year twos," said Miss Reynolds, "I would like to see more manners from the audience please. If this was an opera, those whisperers would get thrown out by the ushers. Now, show Ruby the respect you would like to be shown, thank you." Then she looked kindly at Ruby and said, "The stage is all yours."

She began with a long and whiney "Well . . .

". . . On Friday, I found this little thing on the playground. It's a little creature . . ."

She started to undo the lid, slowly.

". . . and I think it's really weird, but I also think it's really cute. I decided to look after it and when me and my grandma went to the zoo yesterday, I took it with me so I could look after it . . ."

"It's in there is it? This . . . creature?" Miss Reynolds asked nervously, half expecting to have to get up and watch from the back of the room. *

Ruby answered, full of disappointment. "No, this is where I kept it. This was his little home, but . . . at the zoo, I lost it."

She held the container almost vertical so that the class could see the little environment Ruby had made for it in there.

". . . it got out somehow," she continued, ". . . and that's when all the animals from the zoo started to disappear."

---

*   Miss Reynolds was not keen on spiders, and she feared the worst. One of the downsides of being a teacher, was that many children were not afraid of the odd creepy crawly and would not think twice about bringing them into the classroom.

*   *   *

"So the big surprise of where you were going to take me for my last trip . . . an interesting, but harmless place *anywhere in the universe! . . .* is Adelaide. Australia. Earth," Evie was saying, mega-ly disappointed. She decided at that moment never to get excited or look forward to anything ever again. She'd been tricked. It was just like that time when she was nine, just five years ago. She was watching T.V. with her brother James, quite late at night, and her mum came into the loungeroom and said, "I've got a surprise for you," beckoning her up the hallway with her index finger. Evie couldn't imagine what it could be, and she was getting all excited until her mum turned into the bathroom and presented her with her toothbrush with a blob of toothpaste on it all ready for her to use. Or when for years she'd wanted a pet kitten and just about every birthday, her dad would surprise her with another toy one.

She certainly hadn't expected an unpredictable, enigmatic, space and time-travelling, adventurous lunatic such as the Captain to be the one to do it to her next. Well, never again.

When Evie Bamford stepped off the Train* all she saw was a road full of traffic in a place she recognised,

---

*   Here, I must explain that when I speak of a Train (with a capital 'T'), I am referring to an intergalactic, multi-dimensional, space craft. It used to be a simple steam engine with a carriage attached before a rather clever, but modest English gentleman modified it so that it could travel not only off the railway tracks, but also off the planet, in time and outer space. It is the only one of its kind in the universe and 14 from being driven past it every morning on the way to school. "Captain!" she called over her shoulder. "That's not fair!"

The Captain♣ heard her from where he was inside the Train's engine room. What she was saying couldn't possibly have made any sense. As far as he knew, he had just taken both Evie Bamford and Paulo Vistar ♦ to a planet in the Tuba Galaxy where there are many different kinds of harmless animals that Evie would have marvelled at. So what wasn't fair? He rushed out of the engine room, through the cozy, wood-panelled carriage and tumbled out into the open air bumping into the back of them. "That's odd," he said with a confused frown.

"Don't pretend," said Evie, indignantly. But then her annoyance subsided and she sighed. "I suppose you're right. I should let my parents know I'm okay at least."

"No, honestly," said the Captain, "That *wasn't* meant to happen! Believe me . . ." his voice trailed off as he saw something very long, very fat and very scaly pounding across the road. It caused many cars to stop suddenly, triggering several collisions and sending the smell of hot brakes into the air. ". . . and I don't think *that's* supposed to happen either."

---

    year old Evie Bamford had had the unique opportunity to ride in it a number of times already.

♣   The clever but modest English gentlemen who found, restored, modified and now pilots the Train.

♦   Paulo was the other passenger on board the Train at this time. He was not from Earth, but a planet called Serothia which is about 17 million light years away from Earth, so what *he* was seeing was actually quite exciting for obvious reasons.

At first, Evie and Paulo thought he meant the car crashes that had just occurred right in front of their eyes, but then they saw what it was that had *caused* the hullabaloo. Evie's instinct was to run. The Captain knew not to make any sudden moves. Paulo didn't know what to do, for the simple reason that he'd never seen an animal like it before. But if I assume that you, the reader, are from Earth, (unless of course you're not, in which case welcome to this lovely and fascinating planet and I hope you enjoy your time here), then I will assume that you've probably seen one of these yourself. If not in real life, then definitely on a television documentary, on the Internet or in *Peter Pan*. Walking at its own leisure across the road—either completely oblivious to the calamity it was causing, or malevolently prowling the land, seeking out whom it might devour, depending on which way you look at it—was a huge, green and gold, scaly, terrifying, real-live crocodile.

Paulo, seeing the Captain and Evie's reaction to such a sight, said, "I gather that animal doesn't typically wander the streets of Adelaide, then."

When its cold reptilian eyes suddenly looked towards them, Evie's hands leapt up to her mouth in a gasp.

As if smelling her fear, the crocodile locked its gaze onto her and took a step toward the travellers. Then, before the Captain could say "Shooting Star!" the crocodile was after them—charging forward with its powerful, stumpy legs.

All three of them yelped quite uncontrollably and the Captain shouted out, "Back onto the Train! Quick!" He let them pass through first, took one last glance at the magnificent, smiling creature and its magnificent shiny teeth and then sprung up into the Train himself slamming the door shut behind him. He lunged toward the controls and got the engine going.

"It won't be able to get in, will it?" Evie asked in a panic.

"Not straight away, but if it keeps bashing and bashing at the door, I'm sure it will find a way . . . through the hole it makes."

"What?!"

"Don't worry, that's why I'm dematerialising."

"Oh. Well hurry up, before it starts bashing!"

"But the Train's invisible, Captain!" said Paulo.

"Not invisible."

"Alright alright, *not* invisible, but like an optical illusion. Shouldn't the crocodile not be able to see it?"

"Probably won't stop him from bashing into it . . ." then he said, quieter, ". . . in fact, it probably makes him more likely to bash into it."

Suddenly, there was a big *BASH!* and the Train rocked.

"Captain!" Evie said anxiously.

"It's alright now. We're on our way," the Captain said with a flick of his wrist as it came down on one of the controls. The engine room had two main control decks. One was in the centre of the room which had the furnace in its core that occasionally had to be fed with a special type of coal called Carnane Fuel and at which the Captain was standing now, and the other was along the far side of the room—at the front of the Train, above which was a wide window to look out of.

"On our way, *where*?" asked Evie and she started making her way towards the other windows which were on either side of the carriage room. The carriage was beautifully furnished with an old fashioned standard lamp, a bookshelf stuffed with books and two luxurious sofas opposite each other and it was above these where the windows were. However, Evie saw that the shields were across* and so she couldn't see out.

"Where are we going, Captain?" Evie said, hoping for the Tuba galaxy.

"We're going to the zoo. What's the nearest one you reckon?"

"It'd be the Adelaide Zoo."

"Not a very original name," said Paulo.

"Right," said the Captain, "I'll set the coordinates."

"Can't see what that will do," said Evie.

The Captain knew she was referring to the Train's current difficulty in getting its passengers to where they intended to go. "It's because of that tragic, grizzly villain that got in here and tried to get the Train to work when I'd locked the controls up. I haven't had a chance to examine what kind of damage he did.♦ I'm afraid it's made her a bit unpredictable. But we might get there."

Evie wasn't feeling very positive about the Captain's comment which was reeking with uncertainty, but she hated being negative about things. "We could pray that we get there!" she said cheerfully.

"Go on then."

---

* The Captain had electronic shields that could be drawn like blinds across the windows. They were operated from the engine room.

♦ His name was Mallory, and he thought he needed to steal the Captain's Train to escape the time and place he'd gotten trapped in by an ex-partner-in-crime. He'd done untold damage to the Train's navigation system while trying to get it *un*locked.

She suddenly got a rush of butterflies, and it was clear on her face.

"You don't have to do it out loud," the Captain said.

She was relieved.

While she was quiet for a little while, the Captain rematerialised the Train and asked Paulo to push a button that was near him. They could now see out the windows.

"Look at that!" the Captain said with delight. It looked very zoo-like outside.

Evie looked surprised and then said, "Never mind, God, we're there!"

The Captain looked at her and rolled his eyes. "Oh you're one of *those* people are you?"

"One of what people?"

"People who ask God for something and when they get it, they tell God to forget about answering that particular prayer because it's just happened. That's one of my pet hates, I'm sorry. What does it say in the Bible? Ask and it shall be given to you. What did you just pray for? And who then, do you think was responsible for getting us to the right place?"

Before Evie had an opportunity to respond, (but after she had a small chance to smile a bit in realisation), the Captain said, "Shall we go?"

The zoo was a busy hubbub of reporters; camera men; journalists; photographers; tourists trying to see something interesting; zoo keepers trying to control the reporters, camera crew, journalists, photographers and tourists trying to see something interesting; and policemen.

As the Captain and the small crew of the Train walked out unnoticed onto the scene, they realised that about a metre away, a lady-reporter was reporting in front of a camera at that very moment and they listened to what she was saying.

"At this stage, it does appear that the male crocodile is the only major exhibit to have escaped along with a collection of smaller reptiles from the reptile house, only metres away from the crocodile enclosure. The zoo facilitators have managed to restrain the second crocodile from escaping and they are at this moment repairing the damage that was found in the fencing of the enclosure. It still remains a mystery at the moment how the damage occurred. But it has been confirmed that all the reptiles that did manage to escape have escaped the same way, meaning the damage done to the crocodile enclosure is identical to the damage that appears to have been made to the reptile house enclosures as well. The keepers here are not yet able to identify whether this has been a result of human vandalism, or whether there has been an accidental occurrence of some sort near the fencing of the enclosures. Specialist crocodile handlers have been sent for in order to retrieve the animal. Zoo management are certain that the crocodile has actually got out of the zoo, whereas the other smaller reptiles are believed to be still within the Adelaide Zoo's boundaries. They've advised that if anybody should see the crocodile, not to try and catch it or lure it in any way, but to simply keep as far away from it as possible and call the number on the screen."

There was a pause in her speech and she looked like she was listening to something in an ear-phone.

"Yes, certainly," she then continued. "They estimate it's now been approximately eight hours since the crocodile got away, so really, it could be anywhere by now."

She paused again and listened.

"Those in the neighbouring suburbs should definitely be cautious about going outside at the moment. Especially if you live in areas where trees and shrubbery are dense. The zoo keepers say that the crocodile will be looking for moist, grassy areas to hide in and protect itself. Er . . . once again, I'll stress that if you spot the animal, just get on the phone and call the number that's on the screen now and the experts will know where to head. Do not try and go near it. If there are a lot of people around, it may feel the need to defend itself, which means danger for us, so . . ."

She paused again.

"Yep, things look pretty hectic here at the moment, but there's definitely no danger of a crocodile loose. The danger's out there somewhere. Families and tourists came for a relaxing day at the zoo today and instead got this," she smiled as she gestured to all the commotion behind her.

"Hope the croc's going to be alright," said Paul Bamford, standing up behind the couch of the lounge room.

Madeline Bamford was sitting on the couch in front of the television watching the report.

"*. . . are trying to encourage zoo visitors to stay away from the reptile house and ask that anyone who was thinking of coming to the zoo today, to please rearrange their plans, there is just too much commotion happening here as it is . . .*"

"Poor thing," Paul continued, "probably didn't want to be in a cage to begin with."

"Shhh," said Madeline Bamford to her husband.

"*. . . again that if you see the animal, do not try and approach it, do not harm it in any way. The best thing you can do is go straight to your phone and . . .*"

"I wonder where it is," Madeline said. "How long is it going to take to find . . ." her voice trailed off as she saw something on the T.V. screen that shocked, surprised and amazed her. "Is . . . is that . . ."

"Well thank you Kelly for that update. We'll cross back to you again soon if there are any other major developments. To sport now. Rob, tell us about the Brisbane Lions on the weekend . . ."

"Is that what?" said Paul.

"On the T.V. in the background."

"What? It's a news desk."

"No, *before*, at the *zoo*. I'm sure it was Evelyn."

"Evie?!"

"Yes, *our daughter Evie!* I'm sure it was. Wandering around in the background." Madeline Bamford had already started putting her shoes on. "Where are the car keys? Lock up the house. We're going to the zoo."

"It sounds like they've got the situation under control," said Evie, watching all the commotion around her and just about every second person holding their digital cameras in the air. "Or at least, they have plans of how to get it under control. There's probably not much you can do, Captain."

"Who said I wanted to *do* anything?" he replied, also taking in everything that was happening, observing everything he saw. "It's a bit sad that the crocodile was locked up in a cage in the first place. I'm not going to help them put him back there."

"It's an *enclosure*," said Evie. "Not a cage."

"Same thing," the Captain replied with a mouthful of ice-cream.

"Where'd you get that?" Evie said in amazement, pointing at the vanilla ice-cream cone he suddenly had in his hand.

"Back there."

"*When* did you get it?" Paulo asked, baffled.

"A minute or so ago."

"I want one."

"Don't trail off the topic. What were we saying? Oh yes. I have no interest in bringing an animal who thinks he's finally free from imprisonment back into captivity."

"Well how about saving a community from croc-o-dile attacks?" Paulo asked. "It sounds like this is quite a dangerous animal."

"Like Evelyn said, they've got it under control."

"Well, we may as well go then," said Evie. "We could go to that place we were going to go to, before we landed in a place we weren't going to go to until a later time."

The Captain opened his mouth to answer, but then paused. ". . . I'll work that one out when I've got a few minutes to spare."

"Well if it's all the same to you Evelyn," said Paulo, "I wouldn't mind seeing a bit more of Earth, now that we're here. If it's alright with the Captain."

"Of course it is, we're not going anywhere."

"But I thought you said you weren't interested in helping the zoo keepers catch the crocodile," said Evie.

"I'm not. What *I'd* like to find out is how the crocodile escaped."

"Whether it was human vandalism or accidental?"

"Or something else," he replied in a distant sort of sinister way.

"Huh?"

What the Captain had said got Paulo thinking. "Who in their right mind would let this crocodile loose?"

"Someone who's not right in the mind probably," Evie replied. She looked at Paulo. "Unfortunately there are a lot of idiots on this planet, Paulo."

"What's an i-di-ot?"

The Captain sighed, "Many people are not right in the mind. And there are many who at any given time are not *in* their *right* mind. But you never know. I'd feel much more satisfied if I knew the truth about how that crocodile escaped."

"Evelyn Michelle Bamford!" came a voice suddenly from a short distance away.

"That's my name," Evie said, confused. She spun around to see who had called her. It had sounded suspiciously like her mother. She looked for her in the crowd, but couldn't quite see.

Then when it came again, "Evie!!" along with a big exaggerated wave, Evie could see her pushing through tourists to get to her.

"Mum!" Evie called back and ran over to the crowd of people that her mother seemed to be snagged on.

Madeline got through to the clear part of the pathway successfully and as soon as she was disentangled from the crowd, Evie grabbed her into a big tight hug.

"What are you doing here?" Evie's mum asked.

"Is Dad with you?" Evie asked.

"Where have you been?"

"How did you know I was here?"

"What happened on Summer Camp? Why didn't you come home?"

"Is James back?"

"Why must you worry me so?"

"Have you seen this crocodile on the loose yet?"

"Who were those people with you?"

"How long have I been away for?"

"Do you have any idea how worried we've been?"

"Has Tanya from school asked about me?"

"Oh I love this game!" said the Captain suddenly, as he'd reached the two excited females. "Can I play?"

"What game?" they asked in unison.

"The question game, where you have to reply to everything with a question or you lose."

"Who are you?" Evie's mother asked.

"Erm, who do you *think* I am?"

"How do you know my daughter?"

"Would you believe I met her on a Train?" the Captain smiled.

"What were you doing on a train?" she turned to Evie.

"Wasn't it *next* to the Train that we actually met?"

"Can I *please* get a straight answer?"

"Did you want a straight answer?"

"Yes of course!"

"You lose!" cried the Captain—a big smile on his face.

"I beg your pardon!" Evie's mum was so confused.

"Sorry mum, look, this is the Captain. And this is Paulo. They're my friends."

"I've never met them before."

"Well I'm introducing you now."

Evie's mum was still confused, but she shook both the man and the boy's hand for now* and then announced,

---

* I say boy, but this makes Paulo sound like a ten year old, whereas he was actually roughly seventeen.

"Well I'm very pleased to meet you but I'm taking this young lady home now. She's got a lot of explaining to do."

"No mum, not yet."

Madeline grabbed her daughter firmly by the wrist. "I'm sorry that my patience and flippancy seem to have deserted me at the moment, but I have a daughter who's been missing for three days on top of the four days at Summer Camp. And when I asked the youth group where you were, they told me you hadn't even shown *up* at Summer Camp. So please forgive me for expecting a straight answer." She addressed the Captain. "I'm sorry, but you and your son will have to continue your little outing without Evelyn."

"Mum, give me a chance to explain," Evie tried to say, but her mother was already dragging her away from Paulo and the Captain.

There were so many things Evie wanted to shout back to them, yet she didn't exactly know *what* to shout back or what was the most important thing she should get out before they were out of earshot. So she found herself being torn further and further away from them, without saying a word.

Strangely, the Captain wasn't even looking at Evie disappearing into the crowd towards the main gate. He seemed to be preoccupied with something else and so Paulo took the liberty to shout out to Evie, "It's okay! You do what you need to do! We'll come and get you!"

Later, when Evie was in the car, being driven away from the zoo, she was angry at herself for not thinking of the most obvious thing to call back to Paulo after he'd said what he said. Her address.

Chapter Two

A Job for the Captain?

Evie's dad had been waiting at the main gate of the zoo. They weren't allowing any more visitors in while the place was so congested, but when Madeline Bamford had said she just wanted to go in and get her daughter, they asked that her husband stay outside. He was now driving the car; mum was in the front with him and Evie was in the back—being interrogated.

"And where's James? You still haven't explained where James is," Evie's mum was saying.

Evie suddenly feared for her brother's life. The last time she saw James was on a huge Satellite orbiting Serothia that was about to blow up. She felt sure he got off in time via the transmat beam, but if he did, wouldn't he have been home by now? Thoughts of James and Lisa—their friend who was with him—now overtook all her thoughts. She couldn't concentrate on anything else.

"Do you expect us to believe this whole bit about a space-travelling train?" asked her dad. "You read far too many science-fiction books. I mean, if anyone loves science-fiction it's me, but if you can't separate real life from fantasy . . ."

"It's all true, dad," Evie tried for the third time. "You asked me to tell you the truth, so I'm telling it to you."

Madeline looked at her husband. Paul looked at her. It was a look that needed no words. A look that clearly said, "Do we look into getting her some professional help?"

When they'd arrived home, the heat of argument had passed and they embraced her again saying how worried they'd been and how relieved and glad they were to have her back. Evie felt so good to be back with them again, yet her heart was a mixed bag of emotions. She was overjoyed to be with her mum and dad whom she loved very much. She was concerned about the whole zoo-crocodile situation. She felt comfortable being amongst familiar surroundings again. She was troubled about whether she would ever see the Captain, Paulo or the Train ever again. And above all, she was worried to the point of feeling sick about James and Lisa. I don't know if you've ever felt overjoyed, concerned, comfortable, troubled and worried all at the same time before, but let me tell you, it's one crazy concoction!

Time seemed to pass differently at home. For a good deal of the afternoon, she was just moping around, following behind her mum wherever she went, dragging her feet and not being of much use whenever her mother asked for help.

Her mother thought that maybe Evie would get whipped back into reality if she participated in mundane things. But for anything she did, Evie always seemed to offer some thoughtful, uncharacteristic, philosophical opinion.

She asked Evie to help with the dishes and she'd said while drying the cutlery, "I wonder what kind of utensils they use on different planets. You know, whether anyone else out there has thought of knives and forks to eat with."

She was drinking a cup of hot chocolate and watching last night's *Home and Away* with her and she'd said, "Do you think that everyone in the town of Summer Bay is in control of their own minds and emotions or do you reckon that guy has control and is keeping them all there against their will?"

They were out in the garden, pulling out some weeds, and after they'd established that none of the weeds were deadly or slightly purple in colour, a dead bee was spotted on the pavers that a colony of ants had apparently spotted as well. "I'd better go and get the fly-spray," her mum had said and Evie replied, "No don't! Those ants have got families to provide for! Let them get to their homes with tonight's dinner!"

And it went on. Evie's parents were so wonderfully thankful to have their daughter home safe and sound, but they had to start wondering whether she *was* completely there.

That same afternoon, the Captain was making his way through the zoo, with Paulo trailing close behind. Paulo guessed straight away that he was heading towards the reptile house, but he wished they could have made some stops along the way outside the different animal enclosures. Some of the animals he caught a glimpse of looked so fascinating. He saw an animal that was so hairy you'd have difficulty finding its face and he saw animals that had no hair at all. Animals that were tall and pink and standing on one leg and animals that were short and fat and hiding just below the surface of a pond. There were black and white animals and brightly coloured animals. Some animals had stripes and some animals had spots. Some with long necks and short noses and some with short necks and long noses. There were some animals with no real determinable shape at all and a collection of animals in one particular enclosure with blue bottoms! There were animals with long tails and animals with short tails, and when the Captain started to slow down his pace, Paulo saw some animals that seemed to have no body and *all* tail.

They were at the Reptile House and there were even more reporters and camera crew assembled there. At the entrance to the Reptile House is where you'll find the crocodile enclosure. And although Paulo had already started to enter the hallway of exhibits, the Captain had stopped outside, staring down at the bottom of the sturdy fencing that separated the crocodiles from the rest of the world. He was staring down hard at the metal fencing. There was a hole there alright, and the zoo keepers had placed another piece of fencing behind it, to patch up the hole temporarily. But as Paulo looked down to what the Captain was looking at, the answer came to him as easily as it did to the Captain. The metal down in that one section of fencing, looked as though it had corroded. There was a rough, darkened edge right around the hole and some traces of rusting.

"What does this mean?" Paulo asked, softly.

The Captain rubbed the back of his neck and raised his eyebrows. "I haven't a clue. We know how the hole was created, but we don't know how the hole was created . . . if you know what I mean."

"Yes, I think I do."

The Captain squatted down to examine it more closely, but without touching it. "Looks like it's corroded. But by what?"

"Some sort of toxic substance? Toxic waste? Chemicals?"

"But from where? And how did it just affect this one tiny area."

"It must have affected another area inside the Reptile House as well, remember? Some smaller reptiles got out too."

"It's still a tiny area. In little blobs. Two or maybe three little blobs."

After a little pause, they both sighed. "I've got no ideas, Captain."

"Maybe this isn't a job for us. Maybe it's a job for a chemist or the zoo-detective. Is there such a thing?"

Paulo shrugged.

"Well there ought to be now."

"Sorry, this area's out of bounds to visitors," said a man in a navy blue polo shirt with *Adelaide Zoo* embroidered on the top right-hand side.

"We thought we'd try and help with the mystery," said the Captain.

"We can handle it, thanks. We have trained professionals."

"Ah, but have you thought about whether any *more* animals will get loose the same way? If you don't know what's caused it, how can you stop it from happening again?"

"Leave it to us please, sir. Now you'd better move along. There could be deadly snakes loose anywhere 'round here."

The Captain and Paulo were being subtly shuffled away by the zoo-keeper, but the progression was stopped abruptly when the Captain said, "Wait a minute! Wait a minute! What's this? A clue?" He hopped back to the metal fence of the crocodile cage and knelt over a small puddle of wetness significantly close to the hole. It looked (in the Captain's imagination) like a trail of water from the hole, leading outwards a bit until it thinned out to dry ground. "Important question," he said, without looking up from the ground. "Why is the ground wet here and dry everywhere else?" He dabbed his middle finger in the puddle and then examined his finger.

"I wouldn't touch that," said the zoo-keeper, wrinkling his nose.

"Why not?"

"That's where my dog peed a few minutes ago."

The Captain, still staring at his finger, swallowed. "Charming," he said and stood upright.

Paulo reached into his blue overall pockets, pulled out a clean tissue and handed it to the Captain.

Grateful, the Captain wiped his finger and then suddenly looked at the keeper with great interest. "A dog?"

"The dog comes with me on my trek 'round the zoo in the evenings to check everything's alright for the night."

"A trained dog pe . . . relieving itself on the job . . ." said the Captain, ". . . usual occurrence?"

The keeper hesitated. ". . . Well no."

"Then why would it suddenly do it out of the blue, right near the hole of the crocodile enclosure?"

The keeper had a blank expression.

"Even though this puddle isn't really a piece of evidence," the Captain continued, "it's still a piece of evidence that's rather suggestive, don't you think?"

The Captain was the most baffling person Paulo had ever met. Knowing how the hole was created but not knowing how it was created? Not a piece of evidence that *is* a piece of evidence? He kind of knew what he meant, but it was the confusing way he put it.

The keeper was still blank-faced, while the Captain's face was lit up with ideas. "What if there was a new smell? One the dog wasn't used to—had never smelt it before. A smell that humans can't smell but dogs can. Dogs are extremely territorial and this one would have been trained not to react to all the animals in the zoo. But this new smell forced him to mark his territory."

"But from what? What made the smell?" Paulo asked, assuming all of the Captain's speculations to be true.

"An animal it did not recognise as one that is usually within the walls of the zoo. In other words, a strange new creature that is mysteriously and terribly out of place. Maybe this is a job for us after all."

Evie was sitting in front of the television again. This time, watching the news coverage of the situation at the zoo.

"What do you want for tea tonight, Evie?"

"Whatever," she called back, not wanting to miss any of the news. Usually, it was her parents trying to watch the news, and Evie the one making noise and distracting them from it.

"But tonight's a special night! We could have your favourite, only I'll have to get it out of the freezer."

"Hang on, mum!"

A primary school teacher at Eternal Promise Christian School has reported to the police a story of one of her students having been to the Adelaide Zoo yesterday with a small unidentified creature.

"Well I need to know now! Or shall we just have these chops that are already defrosted?"

The teacher claims that this was perhaps what caused the events to follow. Although a very unconvincing story, police are not ruling anything out. Contact is still to be made with the seven year old student claiming to have possessed this mysterious creature, while her teacher, Miss Beth Reynolds believes police should seek outside help and is requesting the presence of a man she calls, the ca . . .

"No answer! That means we're having chops. Will you come and help me chop up the veggies, please?"

"Mum!! I missed it! He was saying . . ." then Evie finished her sentence quieter, so that only she could hear her own voice. ". . . I'm sure he said, *the Captain.*

Evie's mum came into the lounge room to catch the last part of the news report.

Police became suspicious of the young teacher's sanity, when she suggested that the creature must have come from outer space . . .

"I would be questioning her sanity too," said Evie's mum, who was standing behind the lounge chair holding a carrot and a peeler. "I'm not sure she's in the right job. She should be a science-fiction writer." She went over to turn the television set off.

"Stop talking mum! And leave it on, I'm watching it."

The scene changed from the news room to a school yard with a young woman in the foreground with a concerned face.

I don't really wish to talk anymore about my student. She's too young and innocent, I don't believe she should be getting hassled so much by the media. All I want to say while I'm on national T.V. is this . . . Captain, if you're out there, this might be a job for you. So get your butt over here so that you can get to the bottom of what this is all about . . .

Chapter Three

The Taxi

Well, what do you make of that? said the man at the news desk to a woman sitting next to him. He was smiling. She smiled too, *I don't know but I think maybe that teacher must need a bit of a break. All the commotion might be too much for her . . .* They chuckled annoyingly. *Moving on now to the weather. Trish, I hear we're to expect some storms over the next few days . . .*

Evie's mum turned it off then and got no complaint from her daughter. "Is that any way to speak to your mother?"

"Huh? Oh, no, sorry. I just *had* to see the end of that report. And now we *have* to get back to the zoo as soon as possible."

"What? Certainly not. You're going to help me prepare tea."

"But I've got to tell the Captain about this!"

"She can't be talking about the same captain you were with."

"She *must* have been! I've got to tell him to go to that school. What was it called?"

For a moment, it almost looked as though Evie's mum was running out of ways to disagree with Evie. She hung

27

her head and sighed to herself, shaking her head. But when she spoke next, Evie realised her mum had done that because she was worried about her own daughter's sanity and how much she wished Evie would stop talking nonsense—not because she was finally being convinced.

"We're not going anywhere, Evie." It was a stern word, but kind at the same time. "I think you need some rest . . ."

"No! No I don't!"

"And maybe after a little sleep, you'll feel like your old self again."

Evie sighed angrily. There was no telling her. She'd tried her luck on Dad earlier to see if he would believe her after the eighteenth time, but that had been no use either. He seemed not to even want to talk about the subject. For now, Evie decided to go to her room. Her mother would think she was having a rest, but what she was really doing, once she'd closed her door and slumped onto her bed,* was thinking as hard as she possibly could of how she could get word to the Captain about what she'd seen on the news.

After trying to get into, and being thrown out of the 'staff-only' areas in an attempt to find some more clues, and even after dressing up as zoo-keepers to try and get into and getting thrown out of the 'staff-only' areas in an attempt to find some more clues, Paulo had to start asking the Captain some very relevant questions like:

"What shall we do next?", "Shall we just give up?" and "Should we just leave and try to get to the place you

---

* which incidently felt really really **really** good.

originally intended to go after taking off from Planet Zero?" *

But the Captain's appetite had been whetted. Not for food, since he'd just eaten a second ice-cream cone, but for a mystery.

Nonetheless, they were heading back to where the Train was and just as the Captain was finding the key in one of his pockets, Paulo had an idea.

"If we couldn't trick people in zoo-keeper outfits, maybe we could trick them another way. Do you have a change of clothes in the Train?"

"Of course I do. Contrary to what my mother use to think, I do have showers and change my clothes regularly."

"Well what if we dressed up as a journalist and a photographer?"

The Captain liked the idea. And he could just picture a particular collection of clothes laying under the floor of the carriage room that would be perfect for the charade.

"Oh, it's you again," said the manager of the zoo, when they came past with their disguises, notebook and camera-that-didn't-actually-work-anymore. "Look I told you, no visitors are allowed beyond this point. I don't know what you're snooping about for, but you need to mind your own business. In fact," he picked up his mobile phone that was hooked on his belt and dialed a short number. "Security, I want you to escort two men off the grounds please, they're here with me at the moment near the staff

---

* A planet in an unknown location named by an interesting man who controlled a place called The Sanctuary where he was keeping people against their will.

building. They're not hostile to my knowledge, but if you want my opinion, I think they're troublemakers. And really nosey."

And that was that. The Captain and Paulo were on the outside of the zoo, looking in.

"It was a good idea," said the Captain. "Don't be too discouraged."

At that moment, a taxi (among many taxis) was driving along Frome Road, which stretches right alongside the frontage of the Adelaide Zoo. The two passengers in the back were exhausted—looking forward to getting home and having a shower after a long, hard, confusing time away. The female riding in the car was finding it hard to keep her eyes open, but the male, sitting next to her was gazing out the window, heavy with thoughts. His brow was set in a troubled frown. That is, until he saw a couple of people standing outside the zoo that he recognised. Two people that had played a part in getting him completely lost and very far from home in the first place. Two people that perhaps held the secret of where his sister was.

"Stop the car, please," he said to the taxi driver. "Excuse me, can you stop the car, please? Now?"

The jolt when the driver pulled over, woke the girl in the back seat beside him. By the time she'd opened her eyes fully, the young man had thrown off his seat belt, raced out of the car and was now running across the road.

"Well we've got to get back in there some how," Paulo was saying. "The Train's still in there.

"Perhaps if we dressed up as a couple of pandas . . ."

"Captain! Paulo!"

They turned to where the voice had come from.

"Captain!! Paulo!!"

"Do my eyes deceive me?" the Captain said, after spotting the young man running across the road towards them, dodging oncoming, horn-tooting cars.

There was a girl jogging up behind him now as well, just as the young man reached them and said, "I can't believe it. Is it really you?"

A broad smile started working up on the Captain's face as he said, "I do believe it's Jamie and Elise!"

"James and Lisa!" said James and Lisa together.

"James and Lisa!" said Paulo, also with a smile. "I don't believe it! You're the two Earth people who helped us on the satellite!"

And then both Paulo and James said to each other in unison, "What are you doing here?"

"We ended up in Germany!" James said, after he'd paid the taxi driver and told him he could drive away. "The transmat beam on the satellite landed us in Germany. So we had to find enough money to get ourselves back home."

"So hard, since we hardly knew any German," Lisa added. "We've only just got into Adelaide and we were on our way home in the taxi from the airport."

"Now," said James with a serious face. "Before we talk about anything else. Do you know anything about my sister Evie? She never came via the transmat beam and we haven't seen her since that time on the satellite. Please tell me she was able to escape some other way. Or that she's been with you this whole time. She said she'd be right behind us but she wasn't and if anything's happened to her . . ."

"Relax James, relax," the Captain said gently.

Before the Captain could continue, James jumped in again, "But she's with you is she? I mean, if she's not with you, then where is she?"

"She *was* with us."

James started to look worried.

The Captain continued, with a smile that was broadening. "She's perfectly safe. She was with us right here in the zoo and who should turn up, but your parents. They took her back home. She's safe."

"Really?"

Both Paulo and the Captain nodded and said earnestly, "Yes."

James and Lisa let out a huge sigh of relief and James, without being able to control himself, hugged both the Captain and Paulo in turn. It took them both very much by surprise—especially Paulo who, being from Serothia, wasn't accustomed to this particular custom.

"Looks like you lost your taxi," said the Captain afterwards.

"I sent it away," said James.

"I thought you'd want to get straight home."

There was an awkward silence.

"Well I . . . I kind of do."

"How are you going to do that without a taxi?"

Another awkward silence.

"I . . . kind of hoped that maybe . . . you could take us there. You . . . have some kind of . . . transport don't you?"

"I think he means the Train, Captain," Paulo whispered.✤

✤   James had never been for a ride in the Train. His only experience of it so far was getting a sore nose from bumping

"Ah," said the Captain.

"Evie kept on about this train thing of yours. I assumed . . ." his shoulders sank, "I *assumed*. I'm sorry."

"No no, it's quite alright, there's no reason why the Train can't take you home, it's just that . . . it's in there," he pointed to the zoo gates, "and we're out here."

Paulo elaborated, ". . . And we need to think of a way to get in there without being thrown out again straight away."

"Just say you're innocent tourists."

"They're not letting anyone else in because of the situation."

"Then say you're zoo-keepers."

"Tried that."

"You could pretend to be a journalist."

"Didn't work."

"Camera men?"

They shook their heads.

"Well that's me all out of ideas," said James.

"Why do you think she's sticking to this story about travelling in space and meeting baby Jesus and being in different dimensions?" Evie's mum was saying, biting her nails on the couch in the lounge.

"It's too ridiculous for words," said her dad, not looking at his wife in the eyes, but staring down at the floor.

"Too ridiculous," she said thoughtfully. "She'd never expect us to believe something like that. So why is she trying? Maybe there's something in it?"

---

into it on account of not being able to see it.

33

"Unless she's banking on you thinking that and so she's making up a story that's so ridiculous so that we'll actually believe it. The old double negative."

". . . But *why?*"

". . . I know. Why? It's ludicrous."*

Just then, there was a sound that had never been heard in the Bamford household until that day. It was the first time Mrs Bamford had ever heard the rhythmic chugging of the engine. Mr Bamford felt a chill down his spine when the loud steam whistle blew—right there in his lounge room. It also marked the first time James Bamford had ever been inside the Train.

Paul and Madeline couldn't *see* anything, but the sound grew louder and louder and they began to think that someone had built railway tracks through the middle of their house in the last few hours somehow and that they were all seconds away from being run over by an idiot at the controls of an old steam train! But then it stopped, and suddenly, a boy of about seventeen tumbled out of thin air, right there in their lounge room saying, "Two flukes in a row! We're in the right place by the looks! Hang on though . . . *are* we in the right house?"

"Of course we are," said a man, also emerging from thin air, stepping off onto the carpet of the lounge room. "Fluke Schmuke! I wish you'd give my Friend a bit more credit than that."

This taller, older looking man of about thirty, in a long brown coat and old-fashioned driving goggles spotted the two gob-smacked parents in the middle of the room, with their mouths wide open and their brows all creased up. He walked up to them, examining their

---

* . . . which is a word that means ridiculous.

34

facial features. "Oh yes," he said, thrusting his hands deep into his pockets. "This is definitely the right place. Look at the eyes," he said, looking at Madeline Bamford. "And the mouth," he said referring to Paul Bamford. "Definitely Evelyn's eyes and James' mouth. But I reckon Evelyn's got your nose and cheek bones though," he said to Paul.

"Who are you?!" Paul Bamford finally decided to say.

Next thing, another young man slowly emerged from nowhere into the middle of the lounge room. He looked tired, shabby . . . and rather sheepish.

Madeline, at the sight of him, gasped and almost buckled at the knees before she managed to walk over and yank him into a big hug. "James! Where have you been? Are you alright? What happened on Summer Camp? Why hadn't you come home? Why must you worry me so? Who are these people with you? Do you have any idea how worried we've been?"

"Can I have about a week to answer those, Mum?" James answered with a tired smile.

"Let's start with *are you alright?*" said his dad, giving his son a hug as well.

"I'm fine."

"And where have you been?" asked mum.

"Hmmm, where *haven't* I been? First, on the road to Point Turton, then I was in millions of tiny atoms, then on a satellite orbiting a planet called Serothia, then in millions of atoms again, and then in Germany! Ha ha! Where's Evie? In her room?" James started to gallop up the hallway, but he was stopped.

"Just a minute. Who are these people with you . . . wait, I recognise you. You were with Evie at the zoo. What's going on here?"

From here, I won't write down everything that was said between James and his parents, and then Lisa and James and his parents after Lisa had also emerged from the Train, for the simple reason that Paul and Madeline Bamford wouldn't let James and Lisa go anywhere or do anything until the whole scenario was explained. This, for obvious reasons, took a good deal of time and even then, the story wasn't believed. And their adventures with the Captain have already been documented in a previous book, which I hope you have read before this one. The time Lisa and James spent in Germany, however, has not been documented, but from what I understand, this part of their adventure was much less exciting than their time on the Serothian satellite and while it probably wasn't boring as such, it would be extremely boring to read and I would much prefer to get on with the part of the story when the Captain and Paulo sneaked away from the lounge room and up the hallway to find Evie and reunite with her. So that is what I'm going to do now.

While James and Lisa were trying to explain everything to Mr and Mrs Bamford and at the same time, trying to convince them that they were still sane, the Captain and Paulo found their way up the hallway of the Bamford home and guessed that Evie's room was the one with the light on.

When they stood in the doorway and waited for her to notice them, they got yet another tight Bamford-hug each.

"How did you find me?!" Evie asked, bursting with excitement.

"Well," said the Captain, "We have a surprise for you."

"Really?"

Paulo took it from there. "On our way out of the zoo, we ran into somebody who knew where you lived."

Evie frowned, curiously.

The Captain said, "Evie, your brother's alive and well and he's down there in your lounge room trying to explain the impossible to your mum and dad."

Evie gasped and covered her mouth with her hands. "And Lisa?"

"And Lisa."

Evie took off down the hall, but stopped half way and came back. "Captain," she said, suddenly in an urgent and serious voice. "There was a woman on the news. A teacher from er . . . Eternity School . . . no, Eternal Promise Christian School, that's it. She was calling for a Captain. The news reporter said she kept on requesting for *the Captain* to be there. They were her words. Something about a creature that's been the cause of the animals escaping from the zoo. She reckons the creature's from outer space! She said something like *Captain, if you're out there, get your butt over here so you can get to the bottom of it.*"

The Captain frowned. "That *is* interesting."

A minute later, the Captain came back through the lounge room door, followed by Paulo, then followed by Evie.

"But how can a blob, whether blue or otherwise, walk across the floor? And when are you going to tell us the truth?" Mrs Bamford was saying.

"It didn't walk, it slithered," James argued.

"I suppose it was trying to take over the planet," said Mr Bamford, softly.

"Well actually, as a matter of fact . . ." James began, but before he could get any further, the Captain interrupted. "I'm sorry to break up this lovely reunion, but I have to get through to my Train, I'm going again. Come on Paulo. Come on, Evelyn. Would you two like to come?" he asked James and Lisa.

"Wait a minute, wait a minute!" said Mrs Bamford. "Evie and James aren't going anywhere. And neither is Lisa for that matter. We're going to take her back home. Her parents are just as worried."

"Mum there's something weird going on at the zoo and that school that was on the news, and they need the Captain's help."

"The Captain," said Madeline Bamford, pressing her hands into her waist and thrusting her chin forward. "Well then let *the Captain* go. You're staying here. We only just got you back; I'm not prepared to let you go off again so soon. You have responsibilities here."

"Please let me go to the school with the Captain." Then Evie grabbed Paulo's arm and led him forward. "A-and this is Paulo."

"That's an interesting name," said Evie's dad. "It's Paul, but with an 'o' on the end."

"It's Serothian. Come on mum, school's a safe place."

"James, explain to your sister why she can't go off with these two."

"Um . . . er . . ." James was in two minds, which means one part of his mind thought Evie should be allowed to go with the Captain and Paulo, but the other part of his mind understood why his mum and dad would not want her to go. Of course, he knew that the sensible thing to do was to stay home, and above all, obey her parents.

Evie's mum sighed. "You can't go because one: I hardly know this man and his son . . ."

"They're not related."

". . . And his young friend then, Paula . . ."

"*Paulo.*"

". . . and two: you've got to go to *your* school tomorrow and you'll have to concentrate on that. So I want no nonsense about creatures from outer space and trains that make cups of tea."

Paul Bamford smiled to himself.

"I think we should stay, Evie," said James, finally. "You can understand how all this must sound to mum and dad."

"But haven't you shown them the Train? They'll believe us then."

"Evelyn," said the Captain, before anyone else had a chance to say anything else. "I don't want to become an enemy of your parents. That happened to me once before, and it was . . ." he searched for the right word, settling for: ". . . ugly. Your parents' wishes come first. This isn't goodbye, I'll let you know everything that happens, alright." He backed away from her a bit and told Paulo to get into the Train. "And when we're done, *then* we'll come back and make sure your parents don't think you've lost all sanity. I'll tell them everything and vouch for everything you've probably told them."

Evie nodded sadly.

As the Captain stepped up onto the step leading into the Train, he said, "It's probably something really boring anyway. Just some mundane thing I need to fix. See you soon."

"Okay," she said, waving, and she enjoyed watching her mum and dad's faces when he and Paulo appeared to *disappear* right in front of their eyes.

The sound of the Train's engine made a crescendo through the room:

Chuff *choofety chuff choofety* **chuff** *choofety BANG!*
Choofety **chuff** *choofety chuff choofety* **chuff** *choofety*
BANG!!

And after it had faded again and the lounge room was back to normal, Madeline Bamford said, "How *do* they do that disappearing trick?"

"Right, so you're the journalist again," said Paulo putting the camera he'd found in the Train around his neck again, "and I'm the photographer. Hopefully this works better at the school than it did at the zoo." He slid on a pair of glasses that the Captain gave him to wear as part of the disguise. "We could be from *The Serothian Sunrise.* That's the name of one of our newspapers on Serothia."

"Sounds fine. Now when we get in there, we've got to try and find the teacher that was on the news. We don't know her name, so we'll have to ask questions in a way that sounds like we're not asking questions. We're here. Another fluke landing you think, Paulo?"

"I don't know what to think anymore when I'm with you."

"Oh, thankyou." The Captain took it as a genuine compliment.

The school was swarming with reporters and camera crew and journalists and photographers already, and the Captain and Paulo quickly got lost in the crowd.

Paulo gasped and staggered back in surprise when he looked around at the scene. But it wasn't the reporters and camera crew and journalists and photographers he was looking at, it was behind him, where they had just come from. It was the Train.

"What's that?!" Paulo exclaimed to the Captain. It didn't matter that it was loud, because there was so much noise around them already.

"What?" the Captain said worriedly, following his gaze. "Oh! You haven't seen it yet, have you? That, my friend, is the Train. You can see it now because you're wearing my special glasses. I can't see it at the moment, because, well, you're wearing my special glasses and my driving goggles are inside."

Paulo marvelled at the beautiful sight. They had train-like transport on Serothia—but not this beautiful and well-kept. He could actually see his own reflection in the gloss of the shiny heritage-green paint. He looked at the big wheels that used to be confined to gliding along a railway track, and the round black shiny smokestack standing tall over the engine room up front. The carriage was beautifully panelled and he observed the writing that was printed in one corner in black cursive script: *Blackerby.*

"That's just the name of the original maker—like a brand."

"It's beautiful," said Paulo.

"Thank you," the Captain smiled. "But we'd best be moving along."

When they approached the main huddle of other reporters and camera crew and journalists and photographers, they heard a tall man trying to explain something to the lot of them.

"Miss Beth Reynolds has already told the media all she has to say and she's now gone home because it has been a big strain. She's been finding it hard to cope with all of the fuss and disturbance. As for us, we are trying to resume a normal day here for the children. Their learning has already been disrupted enough and I don't believe there's anything else here to see. So if you'll all please . . ."

The rest of his speech was drowned out with mutterings by the press. Then there was a crowd-control policeman who was trying to control the crowd.* The man managed to tell most of the crowd that if they wanted more material, then they would have to make an appointment with the school and its staff, but one particular journalist with one particular photographer insisted on staying.

"That goes for you too," said the policeman, who was looking very tired.

"But we're from *The Serothian Sunrise*," said the photographer with glasses.

"I don't care if you're from the moon, this is *not* the way to get your story. You'll need to make an appointment."

"Sorry, just want to know quickly," said the Captain to the impatient policeman. "The man who was talking, would that have been the Head Master?"

The policeman almost laughed. "Head Master. Didn't think anybody was called a Head Master anymore. But you're right, he's the School Principal."

---

* I don't know if you've noticed this, but as soon as there's ever the slightest suggestion of extraterrestrial activity in the news, Earthlings in general go absolutely potty—whether it's with excitement or over-confident skepticism.

"And did he say that Beth Reynolds—*that teacher who was on the news calling for some kind of Captain*—had gone home?"

"That's what he said. Now please, go away."

"Okay, very well." The Captain came away frowning to himself.

The bell had rung and there were little children playing on a playground nearby making lots of noise.

"What are you thinking, Captain?" asked Paulo, knowing that the particular frown he was wearing was a thinking frown.

"Two things," said the Captain. "One: I don't think this Beth Reynolds would have gone home because she *couldn't cope*, it sounds daft. Especially if what Evelyn told me about her was true."

"And the second thing?"

"Those children on the playground . . ."

"What about them?" Paulo couldn't help smiling, while watching their care-free games, innocent laughter, and joyous singing voices.

"Listen to their singing."

"We're following the leader, the leader, the leader. We're following the leader, wherever he may go!"

Paulo was about to say, *what about it*, but then he frowned too.

The Captain said thoughtfully, "Have you noticed . . ."

"Those words . . . it's what Mr Cameron said about A1 and the Sanctuary."

"And what Mallory kept saying in 4 B.C. Jerusalem." The Captain was thinking hard, his brow furrowing deeper and deeper. But then it straightened out, his eyes narrowed and Paulo wasn't sure, but he thought he saw the slightest hint of a smile on the Captain's face before he said, ". . . Do you believe in coincidences?"

Chapter Four

Back To School

It was around two in the afternoon. Evie's dad was giving Lisa a lift home, James was having a sleep, Evie's mum was in the kitchen and Evie was in her bedroom, writing in her journal.

. . . and I met this man who wanted me to call him Captain. Then James and Lisa disappeared and the Captain said he could find them. I begged him to let me come with him.

He took me to a planet called Ser . . .

"Evie! Come and take the rubbish out for me will you please?"

Evie rolled her eyes, placed her pen down on her small desk and walked sluggishly down the hallway.

"Here you are," mum said, handing her the bag of stinky rubbish. Evie took it, but mum wouldn't let go of the bag yet. She kept holding onto it and in doing so, pulled Evie in close to her and planted a kiss on her daughter's head. Evie smiled. She took the bag from her, but put it down on the kitchen floor for just a moment—to hug her mum back. It was a nice moment. Evie was taken back to a feeling of her earlier childhood—when in the warm arms of her mother, everything was right with the world. She considered how many times over the last few days that she'd wanted a hug from mum and now felt grateful and safe and loved and . . . right. It wasn't so bad to be home after all. Things were far from being settled between them, but this sweet ten seconds was enough for now—they didn't need to say anything. Evie then picked up the bag and took it outside.

The wheely-bins were kept a long way from the back door; Evie had to walk right around to the back gate which led to the footpath on the side of the road. She opened the lid of the bin, lifted her arm and swung the bag down into it, dropping it into its black smelly depths. Then she clutched the handle of the lid to lift it back onto the bin, and with the *bang* of the lid falling back into its place, a lot of things happened in what felt like a split second. First, it was the hand that came over her mouth to stop her from screaming, then it was an arm that firmly grabbed her around the waist and yanked her away from the bin and out through the gate onto the footpath. While struggling as much as she could, she saw a car parked on the street with the passenger-side door open, which she was being carried closer and closer towards. She tried to use her feet as a pair of brakes, but every time she tried to dig her toes into the ground, she was hoisted up into the air—she wasn't very heavy. Before she knew it, she was sitting in the passenger seat and the door slammed shut next to her.

Immediately, she located the lock on the inside door trim, popped it up and found the lever that would let her out, but in the time it took her to do this simple thing, the person who had captured her had already sat down in the driver's seat and Evie was pulled back firmly.

"Don't be afraid," the person said quickly, as she clutched onto Evie's arm. It was a woman, and she made it very clear that she wanted Evie to stay in the car.

After being asked to leave along with all the other reporters and camera men and . . . everyone else, Paulo and the Captain were now standing outside the school grounds, looking in.

"Do you think they're trying to hide something?" asked Paulo, now back in his regular clothes, which were a pair of light blue, long sleeve overalls.

"No, I just think they're sick of reporters," replied the Captain.

"Well, what should we do now?"

"Evie said this teacher was fairly anxious to see me . . . or at least *a* captain of some sort. If so, why would she go home?"

"Maybe they sent her home."

"Maybe. But if that's the case, and she didn't want to, then she'll still find a way of getting back here. So I would be quite happy waiting around here until she shows herself, or until the school grounds are so quiet again that we can sneak our way back in without being noticed. Does that sound alright with you?"

Paulo shrugged. "If you think it's what we should do."

Evie was just wondering how she could *not* be afraid, when someone had just kidnapped her and was holding onto her arm tighter and tighter to keep her from escaping.

"I'm sorry, but I can't let you go, or you'll just run," said the woman. Her smooth-skinned face looked vaguely familiar to Evie.

"W . . . what do you want with me?"

"Do you know where the Captain is?"

"Who are you?"

"Do you *know* the Captain?"

"How do you know that?"

"I saw you with him. On the news, at the zoo."

"How did you know where I live?"

The woman shrugged. "Found you at the zoo, and followed you home."

"If you were there, why didn't you just follow the Captain if he's the person you wanted?"

"Because by the time *I* got there, you and he had already split up and I just happened to see you get into a car with who I assume were your parents and I tailed you."

"Will you let go of my arm?"

"Will you stay here in the car?"

Evie waited a while before answering, looking into the woman's eyes. Then timidly, she nodded.

The woman released her, and although Evie was still a little frightened, she had no intention of getting out of the car now. She rubbed her arm a little where the woman's fingernails had dug in. Then she said, "You've missed him again. He was here not long ago and then he took off again."

Her sparkling green eyes lost their sparkle. "Well where is he now?"

"If I tell you where I think he's gone, will you let me . . . well I'm just thinking . . . mum will notice I'm gone and come looking . . ."

"You're right," said the woman, sitting herself up straight in the seat and starting the engine of the car. "We'd better get out of here."

The engine revved and in a flash, the car was taking Evie away from her house.

"Stop! You can't do this! This is kidnapping! Let me go!"

"Calm down, Evie! Put the seatbelt on."

"How did you know my name?"

"I heard your mum call you that."

Reluctantly, Evie strapped herself up in the seatbelt and after a short while of silence, the woman spoke again.

"I'm sorry, I should probably answer some of your questions. My name's Beth Reynolds and I'm a teacher at Eternal Promise Christian School."

Evie suddenly remembered where she'd seen her face before. "You're that teacher! On the news!"

"Yes."

"The one who was calling for the Captain!"

"Yes. So where is he? I said that to the reporters on the off chance that . . ."

"Well it worked. I saw it and I sent him to you!"

"What do you mean?"

"To the school. That's where I think he must be now."

Beth Reynolds pulled the car over and parked again, now three or four streets away from Evie's home.

"So if I'd have just stayed at school, I would have seen him?"

"Probably." Evie gave her an awkward smile.

She thought Beth was going to get really angry for a second. She hung her arms over the steering wheel and slumped her head in between them. But instead of bursting into a frenzy of anger and annoyance, she burst into laughter.

"I can't believe it!" she said between giggles. "So I did all this and put on that *I'm-too-overwhelmed-by-all-the-attention* routine for nothing."

Evie just looked back at her.

"Oh well. I guess I'll head back to school now. I'll take you back home. I don't make a habit of kidnapping people, you know."

"Wait," Evie said boldly after a big breath.

"What is it?"

Evie hesitated, still thinking through whether what she was about to say, was the right thing to say. ". . . Will you take me with you?"

"I see," Beth started to smile. "Hungry for adventure are you?"

Beth Reynolds pulled up into the staff car park of the school where she worked. The girl she'd kidnapped was in the passenger seat. They both got out and Evie followed Beth's brisk steps toward the Junior Primary office.

Evie had to jog to keep up with her. She said in a raised voice to be heard, "This is where I told the Captain to come. Whether or not he'll still be here, I don't know. He left my house over an hour ago."

Beth walked into the building and went straight past the front desk. Evie's subconscious mind made her feel like she had to wait on the immediate side of the desk. There was a line marked on the carpet with masking tape that students weren't allowed to cross. Evie couldn't go into the staff-only area. She was a student.

"Come through," said Beth, trying to hurry her along.

Evie felt silly for hesitating. But entering the staffroom was like entering forbidden territory. It felt weird.

"Come on, come on," she said to Evie in a friendly, hushed tone.

The staffroom was small and comfortable. Chairs, coffee table, kitchen, fridge, microwave, computers, pigeon holes, book racks, the newspaper, pens, clock, noticeboard.

"Beth!" came a loud voice from behind them. "Hi, what are you doing here? I thought you were meant to be resting?"

It was a lady of about thirty—another teacher.

"Oh, Lynette, yeah I had a rest and then realised there were some things I needed to do. Left some stuff in my room. All the reporters have gone I see."

"Yeah, much quieter around here now. Anyway, my kids'll be on their way back from P.E. so I've got to get back to my room. Catch ya."

"Okay. Lynette. Just quickly, have there been any visitors asking for me in the last hour or so?"

"Not that I know of. But Jean should know; she's been on the desk all afternoon."

"Thanks."

The other teacher breezed out the door with some papers under her arm and Beth was checking her own pigeon hole. "Alright. It's nearly home time. We'll wait 'till my class has been dismissed."

Just then, another older lady walked through a different door, (the sound of a toilet flushing could be heard in the background) and Beth spoke to her.

"Oh Jean, has anyone come into the office in the last hour asking for me?"

"No. Did you have a nice rest?"

"Yes, I'm fine now." Then Beth turned to Evie and said quietly, "That's odd."

51

A bell sounded and soon after that, the air was filled with sounds of chattering, laughing and shouting children. And then chattering, laughing and shouting parents picking the chattering, laughing and shouting children up from school.

Beth headed out of the staffroom door which led directly outside, and out here the hubbub was louder and more hectic. Beth said to Evie over her shoulder, "Sometimes it's a real job getting through the yard at this time of day, you watch."

"Miss Reynolds!!!" three children suddenly shouted and ran up to her, wrapping their arms around her waist and legs. Beth kept on walking, but it was like walking through mud.

"Hello girls," she said with a big smile. "Is your dad picking you up today Chelsea, or is Charlotte's mum taking you home?"

"Dad's coming," Chelsea replied.

"Where is he?"

"Over there."

Beth located him with her eyes. "He's on time today, is he? That's good."

Somehow, Beth managed to get free of those three girls, but as she came closer to her own classroom, another girl ran up to her and gave her a hug, followed by a boy as well.

"And how was your day with Miss . . . um . . . Mrs Damiani?"

"Good. She gave us stickers."

"Oh, you lucky ducks. What did you do to deserve that?"

"Not everyone, just some of us."

"I see. Well, can I get past now so I can get into the classroom? Thank you. I hope you weren't giving Mrs Damiani a hard time Rory."

The little boy shyly smiled and Beth laughed. "You know how much you chat in class, how naughty you can be."

Beth moved into the warm classroom, with Evie just behind her. She winked and smiled at Evie saying, "Rory's the quietest, most well-behaved one in the class."

Evie smiled, but then at the sight of the grade two classroom suddenly, her smile diminished. In the background, she could hear Beth talking to the relief teacher:

"How were they this afternoon?"

"Pretty good. We got through everything okay. I had to send Riley out for a while, and Alex was being cheeky quite a lot, but besides that, it was fine. How are you?"

"Fine thanks. If you want to get going, I can take it from here."

"I *was* going to mark these tests for you."

"Oh no, that's okay, I'll do that."

While they were talking, their voices seemed to fade together into a kind of blur as Evie looked around the classroom—at all the details. The tiny orange chairs, the laminated name tags stuck to the desks, the pencil pots, the children's work that was pegged up around the room, the smells of sweaty jumpers, mandarin-peel and air-conditioning all mixed into one distinctive smell—*primary school*. Some of Evie's memories were good. But many of them were bad.

There was something she saw that brought her out of her reminiscent state, and that was one particular drawing that was hanging up from the ceiling on a fishing wire across the middle of the room.

She returned her attention to where Beth was and realised the other teacher had already gone and Beth had been staring at Evie.

"Are you alright?"

"Fine." She had to clear the frog out of her throat before continuing. "Is this it?" she said, pointing to the drawing she'd spotted. "Is this the creature?"

Beth looked up at the hanging page, stood on one of the chairs to get it down and then nodded. "This is Ruby's drawing of the creature she said she found at school and then took to the zoo. She *thinks* it's what caused the crocodile to get loose."

"But that's a long shot isn't it?"*

"Well I thought that at one stage, but take a look at it. Have you seen anything on Earth that looks like that?"

The creature was a small shape (like a semi circle, but stretched slightly vertically, making a semi-oval) that was covered in hair. It had two little beady eyes poking through near the top and a mouthful of sharp teeth near the bottom—depicted by lots and lots of little triangles sticking out at odd angles where a mouth should have been.

"Children have pretty wild imaginations," said Evie, shrugging.

"That's what everybody else is saying. But Ruby isn't the sort to imagine this sort of thing. She's very down-to-earth, only uses her imagination when she

---

* By 'long shot' Evie meant that it seemed to be a slim chance that the two incidences were connected.

has to. And you can learn a lot from observing a child's drawings."

Evie took another look around the room. "Looks like you're doing a lot of work on animals at the moment. Are you sure she wasn't just trying to draw a possum or something."

"Our theme this term is *Furry Friends*. Looking at Australia's native animals," said Beth, walking over to her desk. "We did possums last week. Take a look at this."

Beth handed Evie another drawing by the same student—Ruby North. It held a very close resemblance to a possum. "Ruby's showing some very advanced skills in visual art. Her drawing of this other creature, I really believe to be reliable."

Evie stared down at the first drawing and frowned. "What *is* it?" she thought out loud.

"Anyway," said Beth after a short silence. "I thought the Captain might have come here to my classroom, but he's not here, so I'd better look for him."

Beth headed back out of her classroom. Evie put the two drawings down and followed her.

At the moment, on the surface, everything looked normal at Eternal Promise Christian School. And for this reason, Beth and Evie thought that everything was okay for the moment—that there was no immediate danger. However, I can tell you that they were wrong. At the moment, they weren't thinking about the bigger picture, they were both at this moment very single-minded. All Beth wanted to do was find the Captain. All Evie wanted to do was ask this woman how she knew the Captain. But while they thought of these things, neither of them was thinking about what was lurking in a stationery cupboard not very far away.

Chapter Five

U.F.O.: Unidentified Furry Object

There were less and less people wandering around the school grounds as parents took their little treasures home and teachers locked up and knocked off for the day. The sky was becoming cloudy and a chill ran through the air as the Captain and Paulo wandered stealthily around the car park, watching the place becoming emptier and emptier. When there were only a few cars spotted here and there in the car park, a new car drove in. And it was the person that came out of the car that gave the Captain an idea.

"He looks like the cleaner," said the Captain.

Paulo caught on to his idea straight away. "Don't suppose you have any cleaning gear inside that Train of yours, do you?"

The Captain and Paulo—masters of disguises today—walked freely and boldly into the Junior Primary office that they had seen plenty of people coming out of, but nobody going in. The Captain hoped they hadn't missed Beth Reynolds when they scouted around the outskirts of the grounds earlier.

"Hello," said a lady at the desk, questioningly.

"Hello," said the Captain, "We're here to clean today. The other chap's not feeling too well."♣

"Oh okay," said the lady. "The cleaning cupboard's through that corridor, and then second on the right. Do you need a key?"

This is too easy, thought the Captain.

With cleaning gear on their backs and under their arms, they were able to hop from room to room, classroom to classroom in search of any clues, and/or . . . the famous Beth Reynolds.

"How will you know this woman if she turns up, Captain?"

"I won't," said the Captain, squirting a table top with *Spray and Wipe.* "I'm hoping she'll recognise me. I have a strong suspicion she knows who I am, since she was calling for me."

"For *a captain.* You don't know it's you." Paulo was following behind with a cloth.

"Well we shall see, won't we? You'll need some more elbow grease if you want to get that dried glue off the table, Paulo."

Evie was following Beth Reynolds around everywhere—always with the same question on her lips: *How do you know the Captain?* But how to word it right . . . ?

♣   In fact, the regular cleaner was in a deep state of relaxation in his car up the next street. At one stage in his life, Paulo had learnt some basic hypnotising skills as part of a Serothian college course called "Handling Difficult People Without the use of Violence" or "HPWV" as all the young graduates called it.

"Um . . ." she started.

"Um?" said Beth, poking her head in all the rooms they passed.

"Well . . ."

"Yes?"

"Well, I was just wondering . . . how do . . . well obviously you know of the Captain then. To be asking for him on live T.V."

"I don't know *of* him, I know him. He's a friend of mine."

"He's never mentioned a Beth."

"How long have you known him?"

"Only a few days really . . . although I can't really be too sure. It could be a week. I have no idea."

Beth smiled, as if she knew exactly what she meant. "Well there you go. If you've only known him that long . . . why should he mention all the people he's met in life in the first five minutes of meeting you?"

"That's true. But what if we're talking about a different person all together here? There's lots of people in the world who are captains of something."

"Long coat, wavy hair, driving goggles, although sometimes those glasses, a gadget for all occasions and is obsessed with The Beatles?"

". . . Yeah, that's him alright," Evie laughed.

"Besides I told you, I saw you both on the news after I'd gone home earlier today. That's why I followed you, remember?"

"Oh yeah."

"There was another guy with you. Friend?"

"Oh yeah, that would have been Paulo. You're not going to believe this, but he's from a planet which is seventeen million light years away."

Beth didn't look surprised at all.

Then Evie realised. "Oh you . . . probably would believe me. Of course . . . you know the Captain."

"Ah huh."

Evie had one more thought in her head that she wasn't bothered about saying just yet. And that was, that if Beth was a friend of the Captain, wouldn't he have known who Evie was talking about when she said *a teacher from Eternal Promise Christian School.* He'd displayed a blank expression when she'd told him about the news report. Could she go ahead and trust this teacher woman just because she *said* she was a friend? *Wait . . . or am I over-thinking this?* she thought suddenly.

The girls had reached a storeroom that was adjoined to the staff room. All the lights were still on, but the room was completely void of people.

Evie went over to the 'compactus' files—those giant wall-sized ones that slide along a track that businesses usually purchase when they're running out of room to store all their paper and stationery and files and occasionally useless junk. She smiled and said, "I'd love one of these in my room!" and she slid the heavy columns back and forth, then noticed a folder that said *DETENTION SLIPS* and shuddered.

Then there was a short, surprised gaspy scream and Evie turned around to see Beth staring into a cupboard, with what could best be described as *nauseous alarm* on her face.

"What is it?"

Beth quickly slammed the cupboard doors shut and leant her back against it—wide-eyed.

"What was that?" Paulo said, catching the Captain's eye.

Without another word, the two 'cleaners' dropped everything and raced out of the room and in the direction from which they had heard the scream. It wasn't a loud scream and so they had not been very far away. Through a window they saw two young ladies. One of them was Evie and without hesitating, they rushed in.

"Evelyn!" shouted the Captain. "What in blazes are you doing here? Are you alright."

"Yes of course I'm alright." She was on the other side of the small room from Beth and the stationery cupboard, and so the Captain and Paulo had their backs to the teacher.

"How did you get here?" Paulo asked.

"Captain Johns I presume," came Beth's voice from behind them all. She came away from the cupboard and approached them with a big smile—but looking only at the Captain.

The Captain turned to see this other woman that occupied the room and saw her big friendly smile. It was the kind of smile that made her look as though she was anticipating something exciting that was about to happen.

The Captain looked back at her blankly.

"Oh, it's Captain Pauls this time is it?"

He frowned, and crinkled his nose up slightly.

"Okay, Captain Georges then?"

He narrowed his eyes, the way you might do if you're at a party with lots of people everywhere you don't recognise and one of them suddenly talks to you and insists they know you from somewhere.

Beth folded her arms, "No one *ever* believes the name Captain *Ringoes* do they?"

"Who are *you*?" the Captain asked.

Beth's smile vanished in an instant. Then her eyes began to sparkle in wonder and astonishment.

Evie answered the Captain's question for her. "This is the teacher who was on the news. The one I told you about when you were at my house. Beth Reynolds."

The Captain's face went from a blank, confused frown, to an eye-brow raising realisation. "Oh you're the teacher who was on the news that Evie told me about when I was at her house?"

Beth nodded wordlessly.

The Captain looked at her—soft, brown hair falling just below her shoulders, brunette well-shaped eyebrows, freckle to the right of her shapely nose, dainty, yet easily-memorable features . . . and he did not recognise her at all. "How did you know my names?"* he said.

"This is most extraordinary," said Beth, very slowly.

"What is?"

"That I should be meeting you at a time when in your own history, you're meeting me for the first time."

"Huh?" said Evie. "I don't get it."

The Captain did not have a trace of sparkle in his eye. In fact it was quite the opposite. One of his eyebrows rose and he looked utterly unimpressed. "I do," he said as he turned from her to observe the room. "You're one of those people whom I have not had the pleasure of knowing yet. In *your* past, yet in *my* future, we know

---

* The Captain sometimes called himself these names that Beth just mentioned as aliases in case he needed credibility, and simply *the Captain* wasn't enough. They were always the first names that popped into his head in these situations, but he had not found it necessary to be using one at this very moment.

each other. I suspected as much. Happens to me all the time. What was the scream about?"

Beth snapped out of her little daze and stuttered a little bit before she explained. "Oh, er . . . this." She opened the stationery cupboard door, and pulled out a little glass jar with a lid on it. In the glass jar was something that looked strangely familiar to Evie. And she immediately knew why. She had seen a drawing of this thing, this . . . creature, just minutes before. A drawing by a little seven year old girl named Ruby North.

"What *is* it?" asked Paulo, gazing in, strangely fascinated.

It was small, no bigger than a large peach and it just sat there, occasionally scratching itself, seemingly undisturbed by the attention it was getting. It had long, scraggly hair that covered its whole body, and true to Ruby's depiction of it, one could just see lots of little sharp teeth tucked inside its mouth.

"It wasn't in the jar a minute ago, I tipped all the paper clips out of here and trapped it just before you got here," said Beth.

"I hope you didn't touch it with your bare hands," said the Captain.

Beth held up her right hand, the one that wasn't carrying the jar. She was wearing a thick hardy glove.

"Always carry gardening gloves around in your handbag, do you?" said the Captain, gazing at the creature.

"There was a pair in the next cupboard along with all the other unsold gifts left over from the Mother's Day stall the other week." She stepped over towards the small table in the middle of the room and set the jar down on it and they all gazed into it.

"Any ideas, Captain?" asked Beth.

He looked at her awkwardly, and then replaced his attention on the jar. "Not yet."

"I've never seen anything like it," said Beth.

"It's not an Earth creature?" Paulo asked the Captain.

"Not to my knowledge. But I don't claim to know about the existence of every living thing on this planet."

"Could be a . . . little rodent that lives in . . . holes in the ground . . . in forests," suggested Evie, her arms folded, elbows resting on the table and her head resting on her arms. ". . . in the Netherlands."

"A small rodent that lives in holes of forests in the Netherlands?" repeated the Captain. "Something you learnt at school?"

"No I just made it up. I'm just reinforcing the point you made. That we can't be sure it's *not* from Earth, as we probably don't know about *half* the creatures that live on Earth."

"She's right," he said to Beth.

"But how did it *get* here? And how, when it ended up at the zoo, did it cause those reptiles to escape?"

"The two instances could be completely unlinked," Paulo reminded them.

Then Beth said, "Couldn't we take it to the Train to analyse it properly?"

The Captain looked up at her with a piercing stare. It was odd that this woman should be talking about the Train as if she knew all about it and the analysing equipment that was inside.

Evie looked up at the Captain. She could guess exactly what he was thinking. She thought she'd try and break the tension by moving the conversation along quickly.

"That's a good idea. That way we might be able to work out where it's from for sure. Or better still, what it *is*."

"It certainly might provide some answers about the zoo animals as well," said Paulo.

"Whatever it is, it can somehow corrode away metal," said Beth, thoughtfully. "Maybe it discharges, or . . . emits a chemical that reacts with metal."

"Only one way to find out. So, that's what we'll do," said the Captain and he then took the jar and carried it out the door.

"Where is the Train?" asked Beth.

"It's outside the gate, in the car park somewhere."

"Well if you'll just give me a second, I need to lock up my classroom."

The others followed Beth and when she got to the year two classroom where her keys and bag and coat were, she stopped dead in her tracks just inside the doorway.

Little Ruby North was sitting at her desk, slumped in her chair and staring straight down into her lap where her hands were fiddling with a lead pencil.

"Ruby!" Beth exclaimed, "It's after four o'clock! What are you still doing here?"

Ruby said nothing and shrugged her shoulders.

Beth came right in and sat down on the desk next to Ruby. She introduced the others to her, learning Paulo's name for the first time herself.

"What's the matter, Ruby? What's wrong? Has something happened?"

"Well yeah, something *has* happened," Ruby replied in a soft voice. She didn't have an Australian accent. She sounded like she was from somewhere in England. "The crocodile and those other reptiles have escaped from the zoo and it's all my fault."

"Why do you say that?"

"Because I took my little pet there. I thought it was cute at the time. But it's what's done all this damage."

"But how do you know that?" asked Beth in a tender, soothing voice. "You don't know that it was because of that creature."

"I've just got a funny feeling, Miss Reynolds. But you can stop pretending if you like. You don't believe there ever was a creature that I found at school and kept as a pet over the weekend. Nobody else does either."

"I do believe you."

"You're the only one that does, then." Ruby sighed. "Everyone already finds a reason to laugh at me, and now this thing about the creature . . . they're saying mean things. But maybe they're right. Maybe I am just a freak with no friends."

Here, the Captain stepped forward to speak with her. For now, he kept the jar with the creature in it hidden behind his back. "Your accent," he said to her confidently. "I'd say you were from . . . Liverpool?"

"Yeah. Just something else they laugh at. Because I talk differently."

"Just ignore them. That's what I did. It really works, you know. Anyway, I happen to know that a lot of good things come out of Liverpool. Things that are laughed at at first, but then down the track, they're loved, respected and admired by people all over the world." With this, he brought his hand around from behind his back and let her see the creature that Beth had found in the cupboard.

Her eyes widened, her face lit up and she got up from her chair. "That's it!" she said. "That's the thing I found. Where was it?"

"Well if you lost it at the zoo, somehow it managed to find its way back here again," said Beth.

"What a clever thing," said Ruby.

"We're going to keep it in here for now and try and work out what it is," said Beth, standing up. "As for you. I'm going to call your grandmother and let her know you're safe. She must be worried about you."

"She'll just think I missed the bus."

"Nevertheless we'll ring her," said Beth heading to the phone that was near her 'teacher's' desk. "And Evie, perhaps you should ring up your mother too, hmmm?"

Evie nodded.

"Let's get to the Train," said the Captain. "And we shall do as Miss Reynolds suggested and analyse this puppy."

"Puppy?" said Paulo. "I thought you said you didn't know what it was?"

"Sorry, Paulo. Figure of speech."

"We've got to wait for Beth," said Evie.

"No, no, you'd better make a start," said Beth, while the phone at Ruby's house rang. "If you don't mind, I won't come just at the moment. I need to stay with Ruby until she can get home."

"Fine by me," said the Captain, and with Evie and Paulo following behind him, he headed out of the school grounds and back to the Train.

"It's so cool that you own a microscope," Evie was saying after they'd hopped on board the Train and the Captain had got the necessary piece of equipment out from an old chest in the corner of the engine room. "The year tens get to use them in science. I can't wait 'till we do that. Only one more year. I would love to have one in my room. I could look at anything. A strand of hair, my finger nail, a piece of fluff from under my bed. It'd be like looking through a window into a whole different world!"

By the time Evie had finished explaining her excitement of microscopes, the Captain had already adjusted all the settings on his and was looking at the creature through the lens, making brief, distant mumblings as a way of replying to her. Then he said, "Ah ha!" but this was not in reply to Evie, but rather a response to what he was seeing through the window to another world.

"What do you see, Captain?" she asked.

"How come you need a microscope when we can already see the creature?" asked Paulo.

"I needed to get a close look at the properties of its skin and fur. The stuff you can't see with the naked eye."

". . . To see what planet it's from!" asked Evie, excitedly.

". . . And I think I can conclude that it is most certainly . . . *not* from Earth."

"Wow, you can tell that by looking at the properties of its skin and fur?"

"Even though we can see it's an animal," he said bringing his eye away from the lens to look at his two companions, "its features don't fit into any of the Earth's five kingdoms."

Evie squinted her eyes to recite them all. "Animals, Plants, Fungi, Protists and . . . the other one. Bacteria, that's it."

"You don't know their scientific names?"

"I'm only in year nine, give me a break. Apparently they go more into it in year eleven biology. What doesn't fit?"

"Well as you probably know there are seven levels of classifying living organisms. First Kingdom, then Phylum, Class, Order, Family, Genus and then Species."

Evie shook her head as though he was moving too fast for her.

"Well our little furry friend here appears to be an animal, wouldn't you agree?"

"King Philip Came Over For Good Spaghetti!"

"What?"

"The mnemonic we got taught. Anyway, what?"

"It looks like an animal yeah?"

Paulo and Evie both agreed.

"We can conclude that it's an animal by answering a couple of simple questions. One: Is it alive?"

"Yes," Evie and Paulo both answered.

"And two: does it move?"

"Yes," they said.

"So it's an animal."

"But you said it doesn't fit," said Evie. "What doesn't fit?"

"Within the Animal Kingdom you either have vertebrates or invertebrates. That's the Phylum—only two to choose from. We can see that our furry friend has a backbone, so it's a vertebrate. But the next level down from Phylum, we have,"

"King Phillip Came—Class!" said Evie.

"Now vertebrates can either be mammals, birds, reptiles, fish or amphibians."

"Or insects," said Evie.

"No no, insects are in the invertebrate category. They're arthropods. But it's funny you should mention insects, because although this creature is a vertebrate, meaning it has a back bone or some kind of spinal cord, at the same time it has features that are found in arthropods. Essentially, it's an arthropod with fur."

"That's not strange," said Evie. "What about spiders? They'd be arthropods and they have hair."

"Let me finish," said the Captain, not unkindly. "An arthropod with fur, warm blood and from what I can see here, it most likely reproduces using a process called binary fission."

"Can you translate into English, please?" Evie asked.

"It's a mammal insect that reproduces (or multiplies might be a better word) by cell division."

". . . A mammal insect . . ."

"Binary fission is how bacteria reproduce. So essentially, this creature can not be categorised as just an animal, since it has properties that belong in the Kingdom of Prokaryotes—bacteria. In other words *not* animal."

"But it looks like an animal," said Paulo, utterly fascinated. "And it ticks all the boxes that categorises it as an animal, we just did that."

"Precisely," said the Captain. "Which only brings us to the conclusion that it is not of this world." He raised his eyebrows a couple of times, giving those words an exciting and intriguing emphasis.

The other two were speechless for a moment. Evie had *wanted* to see something unusual today. She just didn't expect to see it here in Adelaide.

"So where did it come from?" Paulo said, softly.

"And are there any more?" Evie said in a sinister whisper.

"That's what we need to find out as soon as possible."

Then the Captain quickly added one more detail to his analysis. "Oh yes, and it's a good thing that teacher wore gloves to pick it up from the shelf in the cupboard. It's carrying properties that are probably extremely infectious."

Chapter Six

Furry Friends

"Okay, you have ten seconds to be down here on the floor," said Beth Reynolds to her class the next day. "Ten . . . nine . . . eight . . ."

The students hurried to put their pencils back into the pencil pots, push their chairs in behind their desks and find a spot on the carpet.

"Five . . . four . . . no pushing Liam, be careful please. Three . . . two . . . one . . . Jessica was the first to give me eye-contact, well done. And thank you Hannah and thank you Ruby. And Matthew, I like the way you're sitting up straight. Come and give yourselves a Happy Step you four. Now, this term, as you know, we've been talking about Furry Friends in Australia and we've been focusing on one animal per week. Who remembers what we looked at last week?"

Most of the class shot their hands up in the air.

"Declan?"

"Possums."

"Possums, good. We're going to have lots of beautiful drawings of possums up around the room soon," then she whispered to them, ". . . when Miss Reynolds gets around to hanging them all up."

The children giggled.

Then she continued in her normal voice again, "But *this* week, we're going to learn about the koala." With this, Beth opened up a big book that was on a stand, knocking off a couple of whiteboard markers in the process. A little girl picked them up for her as she continued, "Now there are some things we already know about koalas like for instance . . ." she was looking for some children to volunteer some answers, "Jack?"

"They have grey fur?"

"Yes they do, you're right. Hannah?"

"They live in trees?"

"Those pictures certainly give us that clue, yes. Fiona?"

While Fiona gave her answer, Beth noticed three people outside the window who were on their way to the door of the classroom.

"Yes," she replied, even though she couldn't be too sure of what Fiona had said.

"Shall we read now what this book has to tell us about koalas?" She read from the first page of the big book, "Koalas are small bear-like marsupials. They live in trees and only eat plants and leaves. Their fur is thick and usually ash grey with a tinge of brown in places . . ."

"It's carrying a baby on its back!"

"Yes, that's true, but don't call out thanks, Joshua. You know what to do when you want to share something with the class."

Joshua's hand went up in the air.

But by that time, three visitors were in the doorway and Beth had to interrupt the lesson to address them.

"Year twos," she beckoned the three in with a movement of her hand. "I'd like you to say good morning to some people. This is Captain er . . . Johns. And this is Evie, and Paulo. Can you please say good morning to our visitors?"

There was a monotone greeting from twenty-five voices and when they got to the part with the names, it became an unintelligible blob of mumbles, due to the fact that they all decided to say a different name first. Beth laughed and so did the visitors.

She said to them, "Let me just tell them what they're going to do, and then I'll be with you," Beth said and continued her lesson.*

Beth finished the discussion time and set them on a task. They all went back to their desks and the room was filled with loud talking, which Beth had to assertively quieten down. Beth brought the Captain, Evie and Paulo to her desk and they chatted there.

"Have you got visitor badges?"

They looked back at her blank-faced.

"You need badges from the front office, otherwise you're not technically supposed to be in the grounds. But tell me first, did you get anywhere last night? Analysing the creature?"

Evie relayed the information the Captain had discovered to Beth, and Paulo emphasised that the creature was probably infectious.

Beth didn't seem surprised but she raised her eyebrows in realising the seriousness of the matter. "Whoa, year

---

* However, from that point on, she'd lost about a third of her class' attention, because some of them could not control themselves from staring at the three visitors as children so often do without realising their rudeness.

eleven biology rapidly coming back to me . . . hang on, infectious in what way? Is it dangerous?"

"We can't be too careful at the moment," said the Captain. "Obviously, we should treat it as dangerous, in case it is."

"Lucky those gloves were th . . ." Beth froze.

"What is it?" asked Evie.

"I've just realised . . . *I* was wearing gloves, yes, but . . . but Ruby. She wouldn't have thought twice about picking it up. And she was looking after it all day Saturday and took it to the zoo Sunday afternoon. If it's infectious to the touch, Ruby's in trouble."

"And so is every other person who's come into contact with her," said the Captain. "We need to speak with her."

"Ruby?" Beth called over the noise of the class. "Come here for a minute please."

"Aren't we forgetting about the escaped, dangerous animals from the zoo?" Paulo asked, thinking they had much more than this one problem on their hands.

"They have their trained professionals onto that. I don't think we need to involve ourselves there. Anyway, the cause of the problem seems to have gone from there and now it's here. No more animals have escaped to my knowledge."

"Yes?" Ruby asked, when she reached the teacher's desk.

The bell rang for recess and just as the class flinched in their seats—itching to get outside, Beth gained their attention. "Year twos, leave everything as it is at your desk, we can continue this after recess. But before we go out, we need to say grace, erm . . ."

Some volunteers put their hands up in the air.

"Tegan, would you like to do the honours today?"

She smiled and nodded and the class bowed their heads and closed their eyes.

"Dear God, thank you for our food and I hope that we have a good recess and nobody gets hurt on the playground. Amen."

"Amen," Beth said. "Alright, out you go. Ruby, you need to stay here for a minute."

She looked worried suddenly.

"It's alright, you're not in trouble, we just need to ask you some questions about the creature you found."

"What's that?" Evie said suddenly. "On her face?" She was looking right at Ruby . . . and the white spot she'd suddenly noticed on her left cheek. She was sure it wasn't there yesterday.

Now Ruby looked really worried. So did Beth. The teacher carefully held Ruby's face in her hands delicately to get a closer look.

The spot was like a large pimple, but white. Beth blinked, and by the time she opened her eyes again, there was a second white spot, right next to the first one. But this one was oh-so small—like a new one just coming up.

"What is it?" Ruby asked in a soft, frightened whine.

"Nothing to worry about yet, Ruby. Try not to think too much about it. I think what you should do though, is get your recess and come and sit in the first aid room for a little while."

"Why? What's wrong?"

"Come on. Come with us."

They all moved out of the room, first to the bag racks, where Ruby's morning snack was, and then straight to the staff building where the first aid room was. The breeze blew and put a chill down each of their spines. The clouds above had darkened and so there was a grim shadow over the whole school.

Jean, the lady at the front desk looked at Ruby. She was wearing rubber surgical gloves while all the time trying to ease Ruby's nerves.

"Looks like a harmless white-head pimple to me."

"I didn't get pimples 'till I hit thirteen," said Evie, suspiciously.

"Everybody's different."

They left Ruby in the room by herself after Jean had done a brief examination.

Now Beth wanted the truth. "So Jean, what's your real opinion. I've never seen anything like that before, have you?"

"Well it is rather early to be developing pimples, but like I said, everyone's different."

"You can't honestly believe that. It only looks a little bit like a pimple."

"In my opinion it's what it must be, there's no other possibility to speak of here."

"How about a foreign infection, not commonly known to this planet?"

"You're not still on about that creature that Ruby picked up are you? You've got aliens on the brain." She spoke to Beth kindly with a smile—which made it worse. She wasn't being taken seriously at all.

"I think we should alert the parents to check their own children. Who knows, we may have to evacuate the school until this is sorted out."

"There's nothing to worry about *at the moment*. We'll keep a close eye on her, alert Ruby's grandmother, and if it gets any worse, we'll call some specialists in. Your anxiousness is only going to make Ruby more scared."

Beth decided it was no use trying to convince her that this could be the result of an extraterrestrial being, so she decided to pop outside with the Captain and his crew and talk about it with them.

"What's *your* opinion, Captain?"

"I'm no doctor, but I do think it's most likely due to the creature. We have to find out what it is and where it's from. If we find that out, we might find an antidote for the infection."

"We'll have to keep a very close eye on Ruby though," said Evie. "Like the lady said."

The others nodded.

"In terms of evacuation, I think your idea was probably not far off the mark, but we'll need more evidence if we're going to convince the scho . . ." His voice trailed off and his face turned a little whiter as he slowly walked toward an open gate which led to the school oval.

The others followed him and were asking him, *What is it? What have you found? What are you thinking? What's the matter?*—before the Captain finally answered:

"Has this gate always been like this?"

"The gate?" said Beth. "It's been there a long time."

"Has it always been *like this*?" he squatted down and pointed to part of the bottom of the gate. Most of the gate was still new looking—all in tact and well-kept. But this tiny little area—about ten centimetres across and three centimetres up was starting to look worn. The metal at the bottom of the rungs was slightly corroded and the paint around it was chipping off. As a result, a little tiny piece of gate was missing, looking as though a toxic acid had frizzled it away.

Beth frowned hard.

"Was it like that yesterday? This morning?" asked the Captain.

She frowned harder.

"Think, *think*!"

She tried to, but it was no use. "I have absolutely no idea, Captain. I've never noticed it before, but that's probably because I've never looked at this gate in so much detail before. I'm not a person who goes around staring at gates. I don't philosophise about gates and ponder their function and usage. I don't observe bottoms of gates everywhere I go."

"I can tell you what it looked like this morning," said a little boy, who was now standing next to them suddenly. "And it didn't look like that."

"Zachary," said Beth to the year three student she recognised, "how can you be sure of what it looked like this morning?"

"'Cause I had to pick up papers before school this morning. Mrs G said I had to 'cause I got on step three at nearly home time yesterday."

"And you saw this gate when you were out here picking up rubbish?" asked the Captain, urgently.

"Yeah, there's sometimes heaps of rubbish stuffed under the gate all along here. So I spent . . . maybe . . . like ten minutes looking at the gate."

"How sure are you?"

"Heaps sure. I'm sure that I'm sure. It was only this morning." He then ran off back to his friends.

"Oh dear," said the Captain under his breath. Then he said, "God bless naughty kids. Without him, we would never have been sure."

"Sure about what?" Evie asked.

Paulo was starting to understand and he told the others, "The fence at the zoo was the same."

"So . . . we can now be sure that the incident at the zoo *was* because of the creature that came from here?" asked Beth.

"Well yes, but not only that."

"Then what?" asked Evie again.

"Well don't you see?" said Paulo, turning to face the girls. "The creature that Beth found in the cupboard last night has been locked up in the Train in a glass jar ever since then. If this has only happened between first thing in the morning and now . . ."

"Oh," the girls said in unison.

"Exactly," nodded the Captain, with a dreary dread. "We now know there's more than one."

Chapter Seven

Potentially Unfriendly Furry Friends

"Alright, settling down, year twos. Excuse me, Liam, you're already on a warning, would you like to try for a time out? No, I didn't think you would. Try and think about making the right choice now, please.

"Now, yesterday, we learnt a bit about the . . ."

"Koala," Miss Reynold's class answered together.

"And today, we should be talking more about koalas but instead, I need to tell you about a particular animal that is furry, but it might not be very friendly at all. Nobody knows at the moment where this creature comes from and so we don't know what its proper name is, but there is a possibility you might see one here at school. If you do see one, we've got to keep in mind that it might not be very friendly. So for the rest of this week, we're changing our topic from Furry Friends to something like . . . Potentially Unfriendly Furry Friends, how about that?"

A student put his hand up.

"Yes Brodie?"

"What does it look like?"

"Well Ruby's actually seen one and she's drawn a picture of it. Abby, would you like to hold up this picture for me so that the class can have a look?"

"Where's Ruby?"

"Ruby's staying home today because she's not feeling very well. We prayed for her together as a class this morning, remember? And don't call out next time thanks, Matthew. Now, here's a picture of our Potentially Unfriendly Furry Friend . . ."

"What's potentially mean?"

"Hand *up*, Liam. Potentially means it *might* be. There's a possibility it might be unfriendly."

The class made their own comments about the creature and Beth responded to them.

"And we admire Ruby's talent for drawing, don't we. So we know that this is very much what it looks like in real life. Now, we think it might even be dangerous just to touch it, so if you see one in the playground, what do you think might be a good thing to do? Tegan?"

"Not go near it?"

"That's definitely a good idea. There might be something you will do though . . . Cameron?"

"Tell the teacher?"

"That's a very good idea. Stay well away from it and tell the teacher who's on duty straight away. Now I know there's a temptation, especially in some of you boys to go near it and pick it up anyway to show people how brave and tough you are, but if you're thinking of doing that just to impress your friends, that is a very wrong choice to make! If you ignore what the teachers say and sort of, giggle a bit and think *well this thing looks pretty harmless, I reckon I could pick him up*, who do you think is going to be the one to get hurt? Jake?"

"Um, you, the one who picked it up?"

"Exactly. So please, nobody get big ideas in their head about being a hero by making the wrong choice, okay?

This is very important. Besides, we already know how brave you all are in this class anyway," Beth smiled.

Beth so far was the only teacher taking the potential danger seriously. If she had her way, the children would not be coming to school at all. At least for now, all the Junior School teachers were telling their class the same thing this morning. At least there was an awareness.

"How's Ruby today?" the Captain asked Beth later on. Beth was on recess yard-duty and tagging along with her everywhere she went, was the Captain, Evie, Paulo and a little one, only five years old who had insisted on carrying the first-aid bag for her.

"She's at home, I'm glad to say," replied Beth. "Her grandmother said her spots are a bit worse today. She's under constant watch. None of the other children in the class seem to have the symptoms. But I still feel the school should be evacuated until we get rid of the creatures. But the school needs more evidence before that happens."

"I can understand that. Anyway, it's probably best not to alarm everyone yet."

"Miss Reynolds," said a little boy, running up to her.

"Yes, sweetheart," said Beth, stooping over a little.

"I went . . . on the weekend, mum . . . I helped mum cook banana bread. Guess what I've got for recess!"

"Ooh, I don't know. Would it be banana bread?"

The boy nodded. Then: "I made a spaceship out of Lego before school and it's . . . it goes faster than a rocket!"

"Wow! That's cool. Oh look, Jayden, your friends are over there waiting to play with you," Beth said, trying to get back to her conversation with the Captain and his new friends.

"Yep. Oh forgot, can you please open this for me?" He was holding up a small box of fruit drink.

"Of course I can, there you are. All done."

The boy ran away and after uncontrollably smiling, Beth turned back to the Captain. "Where were we?"

"Ruby."

"Oh yes. What do you think about the infection? Maybe you only get harmed if you make direct contact with one of them?"

"That must be the case," said Paulo, "if none of Ruby's classmates have spots."

"Keeping in mind though . . ." began Beth; she was interrupted by another little student. A reception girl this time with bouncy blonde pigtails.

"Ak-kuse me?"

"Yes?"

"I went to the toilet at the middle of recess so I don't need-a go after."

Beth expected there to be more to the story but that was it. "Good idea," she said and the little girl walked off. Beth tried to remember what she'd been about to say. "Er . . . keeping in mind though that Ruby found the creature on Friday last week. It's taken," she counted, "three days for the spots to show up."

"That's true," said Paulo.

"Where's Evelyn," the Captain said, suddenly noticing she was not among them anymore.

"She's there," Paulo said, after looking around a bit.

Evie had stopped walking and fallen behind. She was standing still, looking at a small group of children—mostly boys. The others kept on walking and talking, but Evelyn stayed behind, staring.

"Leave me alone," said a small girl who was with them.

The boys chanted loudly in her face, "*Leave me alone. Leave me alone.*"

"I'll tell the teacher."

"*I'll tell the teacher. I'll tell the teacher.*" This seemed to be hysterically funny for them, copying everything the little girl said.

"Ruby's my friend. And she can't help having spots on her face. Miss Reynolds said she's not feeling well."

"*Miss Reynolds said she's not feeling well.* Ruby's just weird. She talks funny and she doesn't even live with her mum and dad." This one had a significant lisp.

"That's not weird. What if your parents were in a different country? You wouldn't be living with them either."

"*You wouldn't be living with them either.* You're a teacher's pet just like Ruby is. You reckon you know everything."

"I don't," the little girl said back, and she attempted to get away from them, but they followed her. When they realised she was heading straight towards the teacher who was on duty, they disappeared.

Evie jogged to catch up with her friends and interrupted their discussion. "Do you realise you've got a bullying problem here?"

"Bullying?" said Beth, "Who?"

"Those boys who are walking away together over there. They were teasing that little girl and saying nasty things about Ruby."

"Oh those boys," said Beth, recognising them. "They're Judy's year twos. I've talked to them before and I've talked to Judy about them. Something has to be done.

I think Judy's going to have a word with the parents."
While Beth walked over to them and told them they had
to miss out on some playtime, Evie got thinking. She
liked what Beth had said but somewhere, deep inside,
Evie thought, *Nothing will be done. Not properly. They
won't change.*

"Poor Ruby has a hard time sometimes," Beth
continued after the group had rejoined. "Her parents still
live back in Liverpool. And for their own reasons, they
sent her to live here with her grandmother. For reasons
completely unfathomable, that gives some kids the idea
that they have the right to give her a hard time. Bullying's
not usually a big problem here."

Suddenly, there was a terrible sound that pierced
through all the noise in the playground. All the laughing,
the shouting and the singing was sliced through as if by
a sharp knife—by one, long, spine-tingling, grown up's
scream.

The Captain, instinctively, raced toward the
scream, and Beth, Evie and Paulo followed him. They
momentarily stopped after passing the staff building and
paused, while Beth determined where the scream must
have come from.

"The gymnasium!" she yelled and she led the rest of
the way.

They came to a large building, which was on the
outskirts of the oval. Once they were inside, they were
standing in a small linoleum-floor entrance where there
were several doors leading off into different rooms. They
would not have known where to go next if it wasn't for
the plump middle aged lady bursting out of the door on
the left, white-faced and gasping for breath.

"Margaret!" exclaimed Beth, running to her and shortly becoming a crutch for the lady to lean against. "What on Earth's happened?"

The Captain didn't stop in the hallway. He raced ahead and barged through the glass double doors that the lady had stumbled through, looking like she'd just seen a ghost. Evie followed him before he could tell her not to, and together, they saw what the poor woman had seen that had caused her to make such a horrific cry.

The focal point of the room was the large swimming pool in the middle, but Evie and the Captain's attention was on the poor soul, lying beside the swimming pool—dead as a doornail.

Although they'd stayed back to look after the shell-shocked lady, Paulo and Beth could just see through the frosted glass doors. Beth recognised the man as one of her colleagues.

"Robert," wailed the woman. "Robert Banes is dead!"

Back in the swimming pool room, Evie murmured to the Captain, "His skin. Look at his skin, Captain."

"I know," he replied softly. He knelt down beside the body and felt the man's neck for a pulse. The gentle beating under the jaw bone was absent, and so lying there on the wet tiled floor was indeed just a body. The Captain straightened up again, looking at each of the little white spots that speckled his face and neck and hands.

He took Evie by the shoulders, left the room and stood in the hallway to announce officially that the man was dead.

The woman who discovered the body managed to stand up on her own and take a new breath to say, "I'll call an ambulance. And I think we'd better call the police."

The Captain was deep in thought, but when he heard the woman say this, he distantly replied, "No, don't do that." But by the time he'd said it, she was already gone and on her way to doing it.

Suddenly, another lady, also middle aged came into the hallway of the gym building and found Beth. "Beth, you're meant to be on duty out there." She frowned, perplexed at the sight of four very grim faces.

Beth merely stared blankly back at the woman and said with grave seriousness, "I think the time has come to evacuate the school, Sally."

Chapter Eight

Getting Expelled From School Is Not Very Nice

The school's well-rehearsed evacuation procedure was set in motion. All the children were first assembled in lines outside their classroom, then their teacher would do a headcount and take them to the big multi-purpose room where they had assemblies, performances, lunch and recess movies on rainy days and other functions. All the parents and care-takers were phoned by the administration staff and the children would wait in the assembly room with the teachers until they were collected and taken home.

Evie was with Beth as her class streamed into the multi-purpose room. There was constant noise as the loud voices of the children bounced off all four walls making a tangled mess of sound in the middle. No individual voices could be made out. That is, not until Evie came within earshot of a group of small boys giggling amongst each other.

"Someone picked up the ponenshally furry thing," one said.

"Who did? Who did?" said another.

"Ruby picked it up and that's why she's not here. She's got expelled." This was the one with the significant lisp.

Evie's mouth dropped. That was nothing but lies! She took a breath and was about to say something to them—defending poor Ruby who wasn't there to defend herself. But Beth took her gently by the arm and started leading her out of the multi-purpose room. Outside, they could hear each other speak.

"They're putting on a Disney movie in there so they'll settle soon, which means I won't be needed. I'm going to head back to the Captain, coming?"

"Yep," Evie replied. "The man by the swimming pool . . . was he a P.E. teacher?" Evie guessed, remembering he was wearing a tracksuit and sneakers.

"Yes. Robert Banes. He was a very good teacher," Beth said sadly. "A good bloke all round."

"And that woman that found him . . ."

"Margaret, she's the Deputy Principal."

"She phoned the ambulance and the police. What are they going to say? And more importantly, what are *we* going to say to the police?"

Beth did a long sigh while walking along. "I don't know."

The Captain had whipped out a contraption from his pocket and was examining the P.E. teacher's body closely.

"What's this one called?" asked Paulo, who was well accustomed to the Captain having some sort of special gadget for every occasion. "Looks like a miniature portable microscope, but I bet it's actually something like . . . a Heat Sensitive Evidence Finding Unidentified

School-Teacher Killer Detector. Or otherwise called the . . . HSEFUSTKD."

"Actually," said the Captain, peering through the little lens at the poor man's body, "It's a miniature portable microscope." Then presently after that, he came away looking grave and almost . . . shamed.

"What is it?" asked Paulo.

"I should have known," he said—so quietly, Paulo almost didn't hear him. "I could have acted but I didn't."

"What?"

There was a noise at the entrance of the gym building. Paulo pushed through the glass doors to find Evie and Beth. When the three of them walked back into the swimming pool room, Beth said to the Captain, "Well? Was it the creature that killed him?"

"Undoubtedly yes," replied the Captain, leading them all once more through the glass doors and into the entrance.

"There'll be an ambulance here any minute," said Evie. "To take him away. And the police."

The Captain didn't say anything but he was far from disinterested in what Evie reminded them all of. He looked troubled and his brow was all knotted up in deep thought. His eyeballs darting everywhere sightlessly—his lids, narrowed.

Finally he said, "I need to do some more examinations of the body. We can't have him taken away by the ambulance, yet. And police . . . that's the last thing I need."

"We'll have to think of a way to stop them coming," said Paulo, probably thinking up ideas for a new disguise.

"Ruby's at home, isn't she?" the Captain asked Beth.

She nodded.

"If we could . . ."

He was interrupted. A tall man came through the main door into the entrance of the gym building.

"Beth, why aren't you in the multi-purpose hall?"

Within seconds of being in his presence, Evie just *knew* he was the School Principal. He just had that stance, and an authoritative tone of voice.

"I'm with these guys." She realised straight away, that she hadn't actually answered his question.

"Who are these guys?"

"This is the Captain, Evie and Paul . . ."

"Get them out of here immediately. This is a school matter."

"But they were here yesterday and Monday too. They're here to h . . ."

"Since Monday? Look I don't know what's going on here. But I do know that strange things started happening on Monday, and I *now* know that we've had three strangers in our school since Monday. So until this is all over, I think they should leave."

"It's alright, we have visitor badges on," said the Captain.

Ignoring the Captain, Beth told the man, "The trouble won't end if the Captain leaves now. We need his help."

"Beth, since they've been here, there's been a murder. Now I hate jumping to conclusions, but where there are children involved, I can't take any chances. I want the strangers away from here and away from the children. If they are involved, let the police track them down, but they won't be found here. See them out please." With that, he left.

Evie found suddenly that her body was tensed up and leaning back slightly, and she now relaxed.

"Keith Henry, the Principal," said Beth, watching him walking across the oval back to the multi-purpose room. "He's usually really nice. Sorry you've got off on the wrong foot with him."

"Never mind that," said the Captain. "We have to stay here. Or at least, I do. I've got a mystery to solve. And perhaps hundreds of school children and staff members to save."

"If you stay, I reckon it'll stir too much amongst the teachers and staff. It might make the matter worse. Look, I'll somehow work out what to do with the ambos and the cops. See if you can research more about the creature that's still in the Train and meet me back here tonight. In the car park."

"But what are you going to say to the police?" asked Evie.

"And how are you going to stop them taking the body away?" asked Paulo.

"Right now, I honestly don't know, but I'm sure I'll think of something."

And reluctantly . . . *very* reluctantly, the Captain and his crew, obeyed, left the school grounds and retreated back to the Train, where they waited for the night to come. The Captain felt uneasy taking orders from someone he hardly knew.

Chapter Nine

School At Night

It wasn't fully dark yet, but the moon was up and the school was empty. A cool, eerie chill came over Evie as she approached the gates slowly with the Captain and Paulo. The only time she'd been at a school at night time was when she graduated from year seven into high school. But then, there were still heaps of people around the place, making it just like usual, except darker. This school, now, was spooky because it was like a derelict. A gentle breeze was stirring dry, fallen leaves into little whirlpools over the pavers, flipping an empty chip packet over and over across the yard. The trees were playing Chinese Whispers all around them.

I don't know about you, but I find the idea of a school at night time—imagining the silent classrooms in total darkness and the playgrounds left lonesome and bare—creepily peculiar.

"There you are," said a voice that the crew was not yet very familiar with, but they knew it was Beth Reynolds.

She came out from around the corner of the first building right near the gate and greeted them. "I was hoping I wouldn't have to start looking for you as I've left my Train-spotting glasses at home. Come along then."

She took some keys out of her bag that she was carrying across her shoulder and unlocked the front office building. She pushed some buttons on a box on the wall—alarm system security code. After that, they all walked in and the Captain asked after Ruby.

"She's weak, her grandmother says. And a little depressed. But there's no sign of sickness yet—apart from the spots of course. I explained everything over the phone and there's a doctor staying close by too."

"Right," said the Captain. "We have to work fast."

"What exactly are we doing?" asked Paulo.

"Finding clues, so that I can work out an antidote for the infection. And while we're at it, it would be good if we could find all the rest of the creatures that are obviously on the loose somewhere around this place and capture them."

"So you still don't know what they are and where they're from?" Beth asked.

"My research could get me as far as the rough vicinity of the galaxy, but nothing specific. Oh, how did you go with the police and the ambulance? Did you drive them away?"

"Didn't have to."

"What?"

"They didn't show up."

"What?"

"That's weird," said Evie.

"Are you sure somebody rang . . ."

Beth nodded. "Margaret was most eager to get them here."

The Captain frowned in deep thought again. He was sure this was significant. He just wondered whether it was a good thing, or a bad thing. "Well, for now I'll take advantage of that and go and carry out the rest of my examinations. Evelyn and Paulo, while I'm doing that, you have a shifty throughout this staff building, see if there's anything the school knows that we don't, and . . ." he looked at Beth.

She waited eagerly for what her job was going to be. But it appeared that the Captain could not think of one.

Beth made a suggestion. "I'll go for a walk around the grounds, see if I can find anything."

"Good idea. But be careful. Don't . . ."

"Touch anything nasty? I won't." Beth handed him her set of keys for the gymnasium.

"Okay. Meet back in here afterwards, got it?"

They agreed and both the Captain and Beth went outside and then went their separate ways. Paulo looked at Evie and asked, "What's a shifty?"

"A snoop," she replied and looked for the nearest filing cabinet. Files had to be a good place to start looking for information.

The next three paragraphs are an account of all three individual searches for clues. The Captain's examination of the crime scene, Beth's wander about under the stars, and Evie and Paulo's snoop around in the staff office. Usually when one is reading down the page, one is reading about events that occurred one after the other in chronological order, but the events in the next three paragraphs happened simultaneously, which means: at the same time as each other. You could read them in any order you choose and it will not affect the historical correctness of the account. Thank you. Have a nice day.

After jogging across a segment of the oval with Beth's keys hanging from a lanyard, the Captain reached the gym building and unlocked the door. (The third key he tried did the trick.) He headed straight to the swimming pool and tried to examine the poor gym-teacher's body more closely than he had before. He put on some rubber gloves from the Train to do it and also got out his miniature portable microscope. While using it, he thought about the ambulance men and policemen who had *not* come to examine the body themselves and take it away to be properly dealt with. He examined the white spots on the man's skin carefully and knew without a doubt that they were a result of the creature he had bottled up in the Train. He noticed the man's skin. It was not only all covered in spots but also very dry—especially his lips. But, he could not quite see what it was precisely that had *killed* the man—the cause of death, as they say in Murder Mystery Land. He thought of the creature they had captured, and then looked around the rest of the room, remembering that there was at least another one of those creatures on the loose somewhere. He stood up and crept around the room, stooping over and looking at the floor, with the microscope held up to his eye. The view through the magnifying lens got more and more interesting the closer he got towards the water in the pool, and finally, he stood up straight, took the microscope away from his eye and said to himself with some regret, "Of *course*."

Beth walked across the oval from the office building where there were no outside lights to light her way. It was dark and gloomy and when the breeze blew, she thought she

heard noises. But of course, it was all in her imagination.*
The far end of the oval was thick with plants and trees. It
seemed a good place to start looking for something that
might be trying to hide. She knew this garden well; she'd
spent quite a lot of time telling children not to play in it
through the average week. But in the dark, somehow it
had a different, ominous existence. For a while, everything
seemed to be normal. Trees, grass, dirt, fallen leaves, a
screwed up piece of plastic cling-wrap. But when she
reached a certain place, in a certain part of the garden,
after a certain amount of looking around, she found a
certain object—about the size of a double bed, but more
the shape of an upturned saucer. At the sight of this
certain object, that looked extremely and undoubtedly
out of place, Beth said to herself, "That explains a lot."

"I feel very uncomfortable doing this," said Paulo as he
watched Evie searching through the first filing cabinet.

Evie agreed but she told him (and herself) that it
was for the greater good—protecting the school from
the creature and all that. "These are all just forms in
here. Uniform policies, TRT documents, fire drill
procedures . . ."

Paulo was searching a nearby drawer. "Class lists,
name tags, report proformas . . ."

"Staff personal details, children with special needs,
dietary requirements . . ."

"Sports Day information, Year Four Excursion
consent forms, Yard Duty roster . . ."

---

* For even though what she was about to find was very very
spooky, it was completely soundless.

"Reading lists, overdue library books, assembly songs . . ."

"Absentee lists, phone messages, ah ha . . ."

"Ah ha? Ah ha what?" Evie came over to the drawers where Paulo had been searching. He had straightened up and was holding a single sheet of paper.

"It seems to be some kind of report."

Evie took hold of the page with one hand, so they could each hold one side of it. "Robert Banes," she read. "That's him. The guy who died. What does it say . . ." She scanned over the page. She'd never got the hang of skim-reading—now was her chance to practise. ". . . Time of death, between ten o'clock and half past ten. Sounds like they had a doctor come and examine him," Evie said.

"You're right. Look down here." Paulo pointed to the bottom of the page. "There's a signature by a Doctor Ronald Floyd. I thought Beth said no one came for the body."

"Maybe a doctor came to pronounce him dead, and they told him the ambulance was on its way so he left again, leaving the rest up to them."

"That must be it," said Paulo and then returned his attention to the report. "Look, it describes the state of the body, unidentified spots on skin, localised bruising on left side of body, likely from fall . . ."

"And look, there's an estimated cause of death . . ."

"Estimated cause of death," Paulo read, "subject to forensic tests . . . dehydration."

Paulo and Evie exchanged a puzzled look at each other—before they both felt something strange come over them. A strange, unsettling feeling that they weren't the only two people in the room anymore.

Evie, thinking for a second that it could have been Beth, turned around quickly—and found that she was wrong.

At the same time, Paulo, thinking that it was probably the Captain, turned around with the one-page report in his hand—and found that *he* was wrong.

Of course, you and I know that it couldn't possibly have been Beth Reynolds or the Captain, because you and I know that the Captain is examining the crime scene and Beth is wandering around under the stars, picking up a piece of litter. So it's only logical that there was a fifth person at the school that evening. And that, of course, was the case.

Evie and Paulo found themselves looking at a tall shadowy man in a hat and a long beige coat. His face was indeterminable, as the light was very dull in that front office and he had his head tilted down so that his hat was covering half his face. Somehow, Evie and Paulo had a queer feeling he was looking straight at them. And shortly, with a start, they realised he *was*, when they suddenly saw the whites of his eyes peering through the shadow of his hat. Almost as though he was deliberately building up suspense, he kept this still, sinister pose by the doorway for a good few seconds.

Until at last, he spoke. "What are you kids doing here?" His Aussie accent was very prominent—like he was from the outback or something.

"Er . . . um . . ." said Paulo.

"Um . . . er . . ." said Evie.

"We're with a couple of friends. One of them works here and the other . . . er . . . we're here on very important business."

"W-what are *you* doing here?" Evie said, trying to sound official.

Completely ignoring Evie's question, the man lifted his head and said, "I'm going to ask you one more time what you're doing here. And I would think very very hard about what I was going to say if I were you. Because *I*," he held up a little identification wallet, "am Detective John Quest. *This* is the scene of a crime and in my experience, the criminals almost *always* return to the scene of their crime."

Chapter Ten

Knock, Knock . . . Who's There?

"I shall have to hold you here as formal suspects while I make the necessary investigations," Detective John Quest continued.

"Hang on," Evie said with a sudden realisation of what was going on. "We're not criminals!"

Paulo said, "We're here to investigate, just like you are."

"A likely story," said the detective sarcastically, walking further into the room. He walked with a little swagger, making him look totally in control of the situation. He was looking straight ahead at Evie and Paulo as though he was assessing their every move and expression, but in doing this, he tripped over the little bin that was on the floor when he came towards them. After he recovered, he acted as though that was exactly what was meant to have happened.

"Now," he said, and sniffed, "I need you to stay here while I go and examine the body."

"The Captain's already doing that," said Paulo.

Evie shushed him.

"Who's this Captain?" said Detective John Quest.

"Look," said Evie, changing the subject, "if you leave to examine the body, how are you going to keep us in here? We could run away."

There was a pause. "Well . . . you can't, because you need to stay here." He walked over to pass them and started heading for the inner door—the one that led into the school yard.

"I think what Evie means, is how can you be sure we'll stay here like you've told us to?"

The detective stopped and looked unsure of himself. "Oh, well, if I go and . . . oh I see what you mean, I won't be here to make sure you don't do a runner."

They nodded.

"Don't you have colleagues with you?" said Paulo.

"A detective sergeant?" said Evie.

"No. Just me. So . . . wait, if I go to examine the body . . . you'll have to come with me, come on . . . no, that's no good because . . . if you go anywhere you might secretly disturb some evidence . . . but if you stay here, you might do the same . . . or, how about I stay with you, and . . . no, who examines the body? No. I'll stay here with one of you and the other one can go to examine . . . no, that's no good. You bring the body back here, and . . . no that's awful, we won't do that. If I leave the room . . . then you two can . . . no. You go and . . . no. I think the second option was the best, you both come with me to examine the body . . . where is the body?"

He almost got the chance to lead both of them out of the room with him, but when the detective finally opened the door, the Captain was on the other side.♣

♣ Because as you should have suspected by now, we're in chronological order again.

"Captain!" said Paulo.

"Paulo!" said the Captain. "Evie!"

"Captain!" Evie replied. "Did you find anything?"

"Oh er . . . no. Not really. Who's this then?" said the Captain, looking Detective John Quest up and down.

"I'm Detective John Quest. And you're under a rest."

"Under a rest? Or do you mean 'under arrest'?"

"Yes. That's what I said."

"On what charge?"

"Murder. You have been found at the scene of a crime, alone, at night. There's no other reason why you'd be in such a place at this time if it wasn't to do with the murder."

"I *told* you," said Paulo. "We're investigating the crime too."

The Captain gently shushed him, placing a hand on his shoulder.

"How did you find out about the murder, Detective John Quest?"

"I was . . . called. By the school. I would have thought that was obvious."

"But why are you here now, and not sooner? And where's your team?"

Evie piped up. "I asked that. I thought of that question."

"Good question it is, too." The Captain leaned closer towards the detective. "And when you say *Detective John Quest* . . ."

"Yes?"

"Detective *what*?"

"What?"

"What sort of detective are you?"

The man's face stiffened. "I think *I* will be asking the questions, Mr . . ."

"Captain."

"Mr. Captain. Now, let's get down to business. I think I'd better interview you first."

"Interview?" said Paulo.

"Yes. You are all my suspects and so I will need to interview you. Separately."

Just then, a fifth person entered the staff room. It was Beth and she inquired as to what was going on. She was introduced to the detective by the Captain and he said it all as though it was a game—as though he was humouring the man in the hat and long coat.

"Ah," said the detective to the teacher, "so you've been out examining clues as well I suppose. Found anything interesting?"

". . . Nothing. Absolutely nothing. No luck whatsoever."

"And yet we've got this," said the detective, snatching the one-page report out of Paulo's hand and reading from it. "Estimated cause of death, subject to forensic tests: de-hidration." He pronounced the word 'dehydration' in a funny way—as though he didn't know the word and wasn't sure where to put the emphasis.

"Right," the detective continued, stuffing the report into his pocket. "I'll talk to Mr. Captain first. And then er . . ." he was looking at Beth.

"Miss Reynolds."

"Miss Rrrrreynolds," he repeated. "And then you two . . . kids. But first of all, the three I am *not* interviewing must wait in this room here," he pointed to a door on his right, then paused, leaned over to open the door, found it was a toilet and closed it again. "No . . ." he walked over to another door on the right, opened it, flicked on the light and then continued, "this room here, while I interview Mr. Captain. Come on, in you go."

It looked as though the room they were hustled into was a little room used for private tutoring and music lessons. There was no way out except through the door they had used to get in. Evie and Paulo smirked at each other and chuckled at the detective's almost comic behaviour.

"He's the funniest detective *I've* ever seen," said Evie. Even though she'd only seen detectives on T.V. up until now.

Beth could understand why they were laughing. But she wasn't. She narrowed her eyes and looked at the closed door where the detective had been standing a few seconds ago. "He certainly is odd."

"Your friend tells me you were examining the body," said Detective John Quest to the Captain. They had sat down at a small table—facing each other. A make-shift interrogation set-up.

"That's correct."

"Who are you exactly?"

"You may call me Captain."

"Yes, I already know that," Detective Quest replied, scratching his forehead. "How did the body come to be there?"

"Well, he was a P.E. teacher and he was found in the gymnasium building. I assumed he had been in there naturally, since the gym is a big part of his job, and it was there that he died."

"From de-hidration, yes we now know that. But what is it that caused the de-hidration?"

". . . Aren't you supposed to be able to work that out?"

"Did you know that withholding information from a police officer is a criminal offence?"

"Did you know that *impersonating* a police officer is a criminal offence as well?"

"What's that supposed to mean?"

"What do *you* mean by keeping us here under arrest without a warrant?"

". . . I will show you my warrant just as soon as . . ."

"You lose!"

"Pardon?"

"The question game . . . wasn't it?"

A little later, Detective Quest requested to speak with Beth Reynolds.

"Miss Beth Reynolds," he began, "where were you when I arrived on the premises earlier?"

"I was walking around on the oval," she answered truthfully.

"Why?"

". . . To . . . get some fresh air," she answered untruthfully.

"Why are you here at your workplace so late after hours anyway?"

"I had a lot of work to do," she said, telling the half-truth.

Knock knock knock, came a gentle sound on a door near them.

"What's that knocking sound?" asked the detective.

Beth shrugged, "Sounds like the Captain might be . . . checking the walls."

"Checking the walls? For what?"

She shrugged again. "Termites? We've definitely got a pest problem in the school. That's another reason we're here. To sort it out."

"So you're pest controllers?"

"In a sense, yes."

"What are you doing, Captain?" asked Evie, looking up at him from where she was standing. Evie was on the floor, and the Captain was standing on a chair, tapping, patting and knocking on the wall and putting his ear against it as he did so.

"Just checking the walls."

"I was right then," said Beth as she entered the little room. "Paulo, Detective Dopey wants to see you next."

Paulo left the room, a little nervously.

"What do you expect to find in the walls?" asked Beth.

"Our roaming pests," he began in a hushed voice, so the detective wouldn't be able to hear, "seem to be quite destructive of metal fences and gates, I was just wondering whether they're affecting the building structures at all. Might tell us a little more about them."

"Anything?" asked Evie.

"All seems quite normal, but I'd better check everywhere."

Paulo sat down opposite Detective John Quest.

"Name?"

"Paulo Vistar."

"And where are you from?"

"Serothia."

Paulo expected to be asked where on Earth this was, but the question didn't arise.

"Do you attend this school?"

"No. I don't attend any school."

Knock knock knock.

"So you wouldn't know whether any strange occurrences were happening?"

"Not really. I don't know what's normal and what's not."

"Not even any strange happenings that were occurring?"

". . . Nnnno."

Knock knock.

"Where were you at the time the victim was killed, which was approximately," he glanced at the report quickly, "between ten o'clock and half past ten AM . . . After Morning . . . ?"

"I was with my friends in there." He gestured to the little room off to the side where the Captain was checking the walls.

"You were in that room with your friends?"

"No, my friends, *who are in there*, and I were out in the school yard somewhere. Near Beth Reynolds' classroom I think."

"So . . . the people in that room are the friends you are referring to, but at the time the victim was killed, you were not in that room there, but out in the school yard somewhere, near Beth's Reynolds' classroom you think?"

"Yes."

"So you're saying you aren't responsible for killing him?"

"Yes. Of course I am."

"Of course you are responsible for killing him?"

"No, of course I am saying we're *not* responsible!" This was the most exasperating conversation Paulo had ever had with anyone. It was like talking to a dumb computer.

Next, the detective was sitting opposite Evie.

"So, Miss Evelyn Bamford, do you attend this school?"

"No."

"So what are you doing here?"

Knock knock.

Evie hesitated in answering. She wasn't sure how much she was supposed to say. "We're . . . trying to . . ."

"What have you discovered that requires you to be here at school at this time of night?"

By now, it was dark outside and Evie was starting to feel tired.

"Look," she said, "there's this creature."

"Creature?"

"That's probably not from this planet and the Captain thinks that it might be spreading some sort of infection."

"How did it get here?"

"We don't know that yet."

"I don't believe one word of this," he said, folding his arms and leaning back on his chair. In the same breath, he asked, "Have you seen this creature?"

Evie nodded.

"I believe you're making up stories to get yourself out of trouble Miss Evelyn Bamford. How big is it?"

Evie represented the approximate size of the one she'd seen, by holding her hands out, about five centimetres apart.

"This is all a ridiculous story . . . is it only the one creature?"

Evie shook her head. "We know there's at least one more. The Captain says there could be lots. We're all in danger. That's why the school was evacuated today."

Knock knock knock.

"I think it's about time I see the body in the gym."

Detective John Quest called the rest of his suspects into the main part of the staff room where he and Evie were.

"Now," he began, thinking he was Hercule Poirot . . . or a school Head Master or something. "It appears to me that you've all told a different part of the story. And one of you has even tried to tell me silly little tales of creatures from outer space."

The suspects all looked at each other, wondering which one of them it was.

Knock knock knock.

"You must now tell me the absolute truth. The whole story. From start to finish. Top to bottom. Left to right. North to South. East to West. No, West to East. Up and down. All over. Through highs and lows. Through rain or shine. For better or worse. In sickness and in health. From ashes to ashes and dust to dust and all that."

Evie tried to suppress a giggle.

Knock knock knock.

"Otherwise, you'll have to accompany me to the station where you'll be in a heap of trouble, and that won't be at all fun, I can tell you that."

Knock knock.

"We'll tell you the truth," said Paulo, "if you won't accuse us of being crazy."

"Don't interrupt. Now if Mr Captain will kindly join us again—I think termites are the least of our troubles—then we can all proceed to the gym building where I will further my investigations."

Evie glanced at the Captain. The Captain glanced back at her.

"The Captain's here," Evie said out loud.

"Ah! So he is. In that case, we can depart immediately. At once, directly, straight away, without delay. Follow close behind. Any wanderers and you're straight down the 'nick'."

Knock knock knock.

The Captain didn't move an inch to satisfy the requests of the detective. He merely stared back at him with his big, blue eyes and said, "You don't understand, detective. If I'm in here, with you . . . then who's knocking?"

Knock. Knock. Knock.

Chapter Eleven

'We Must Survive'

Knock knock . . .
Knock knock . . .

All that could be heard in between the gentle, timid knocking was the ticking of the wall clock as the five stared at the outer door from which the sound was coming. They froze for a good half a minute—almost as though they were waiting, for the knock to sound again.

And when it did, Evie's stomach jumped and then sank into a worried tension.

It was the Captain who moved first. He walked towards the door confidently thinking, *whoever it is, they're polite enough to knock, so it can't be that bad.* He grabbed hold of the round door handle and stopped for a couple of seconds. Then he twisted it, and cautiously opened the door . . .

Whatever the Captain may have been expecting, I think I can say with confidence that he wasn't expecting to see little Ruby North staring back up at him from the threshold. She looked tired—to the point of collapsing. Distant, but fully alert, and no spots on her face.

"Ruby?" Beth said in surprise and she got up from her chair and came over.

The Captain, still holding onto the door handle and not taking his eyes off Ruby, said to Beth, "You might want to stay back."

Beth stopped where she was—halfway across the room. "What are you doing here?" she asked her small blonde-haired student. "How did you get here?"

"Snuck out," Ruby replied simply, having faced her teacher. "Walked."

"You should be home resting."

"No. Where are all the school children?"

"Well they're . . . they're all at home. It's night time Ruby, they're probably getting ready for bed about now."

"No good," Ruby replied simply, finally taking her eyes off Beth. "We must survive."

"What did you say?" Beth replied.

"Miss Reynolds, I'll handle this," said the Captain, looking first at Beth and then back to Ruby. He asked her with authority, "What did you say?"

Ruby showed no wish to speak further.

Evie said softly from behind the group, "Maybe she could get some rest here."

"Good idea," said the Captain, not taking his eyes off Ruby from now on. "Miss Reynolds, where's the nearest sick room?"

"Through here. And it's not a *sick* room, it's a *first aid* room."

"Sick room, first aid room, same thing. Evelyn, take her in there, please."

"Aye aye, Captain."

The Captain was first surprised at Evie's reply, but then he shrugged, turned down the corners of his mouth and nodded. He quite liked the sound of that, and he continued serving out his orders. "But don't touch her skin. Just in case."

"No!" Ruby said as she was dragged into the first aid room. "We mustn't rest. We must survive!"

Once she was shut in there, they all stared in through the large glass window, worried.

"Whatever's infected her," said the Captain, "seems to have taken over her mind as well. The sick room will act as quarantine. So nobody is to go in there under any circumstances, is that clear?"

They all nodded. Except of course for Detective Quest who was sitting in a chair a little distance away from everyone else. He was watching everything. Especially poor Ruby.

Beth Reynolds had been thinking of what she had found on the edge of the school oval and knew that the Captain needed to know about it. She started speaking in a hushed voice so that the Captain could hear but the detective could not. "Captain, now might be a good time to tell you about what I found while I was on my walk. I didn't want to say anything before with that so-called detective around but I think you ought to see it . . ."

She stopped. She could tell the Captain wasn't listening. He was staring into the first aid room at Ruby and frowning.

The little innocent Ruby, had turned on the tap so that there was water gushing at full speed into the sink and splashing up onto the tiles and bench on either side. She sat herself down on the bed, rested her elbows on her knees, and her chin in the cups of her hands—staring at the blasting flow of water.

The Captain spoke softly, sending his words over his shoulder, so he could still keep his eye on Ruby. "What did you say was the cause of that teacher's death?"

Evie answered him, "Dehydration."

In the Captain's mind was a puzzle. And at that moment, a few more pieces were slotting into place.

Chapter Twelve

Unveiling

The Captain was running. Paulo, Beth and Detective John Quest were following him. They had no idea where he was going, but the Captain seemed to have a plan.

He had told Evie to stay behind in the staff room and keep an eye on Ruby—observe what she does and make sure she stays locked in the little first aid room. She had replied "Aye aye Captain!" again with a big smile and he'd left her to it.

Running close behind him were Paulo and Beth. Beth was all the time trying to tell him something but couldn't seem to get a word in. Detective John Quest was a little further back because he couldn't seem to run properly. It was a funny stilted run, as though he'd had some kind of history involving a fall, an operation of some sort, or a fight in a war.* Or perhaps it was some other

---

* When elderly men or hotel managers have trouble with their leg, or are trying to explain their way out of an awkward situation, they often say "Got a bit of shrapnel in the old leg from the Korean War' . . . although Quest didn't look old enough to have been in a war. So it was more likely a wound from his police duties.

121

unknown reason why he couldn't run like your average young and fit human being. He didn't like not being in the lead. He didn't like not being in control. He called out a few times, "I still have some questioning to do! You are all under arrest until my backup arrives! You are all forbidden to run away from the office building . . . You are forbidden to go near that building . . ." and then: "You are forbidden to go inside that building . . . You are forbidden to open that door! . . . You are not to go near that swimming pool! I forbid it!"

He was wasting his breath. When he caught up with him, the three of them were standing near the edge of the swimming pool looking down into it.

"Ah, here's the body," said Detective Quest.

"Yes, you can examine it now," said Paulo.

"Shouldn't we . . . move him or something," said Beth, looking awkwardly at her former colleague. "It's awful just leaving him here. Why haven't the ambulance come?"

"I think I've got a fair idea," the Captain said, quietly.

Then Detective Quest said something sensible. "I'll help you move him if you like. I've seen what I need to see. Where to?"

"His office is just across the hall. Perhaps he could go in there until some undertakers can come. We'll have to call them in the morning."

The Captain let them go ahead with that and Paulo came up to his side while he was still staring down into the pool.

"Don't get too close," said the Captain, softly. "Why didn't I think before?" This was said more to himself than to Paulo.

"Think of what? What's going on? Are we in terrible danger?"

The Captain didn't answer. But he did eventually explain his thoughts to Paulo. "I know what this . . . this *pest* needs to survive. According to the one or many that have possessed Ruby, all they want to do is survive, so that will be what they're after."

Paulo was beginning to see. "So if that man was killed by one of them . . . well, he was dehydrated. And the water in the first aid room. They need water don't they."

"They don't just need water to survive, Paulo. They live in water. I don't think they can exist out of water."

"But what about the one in the Train? That was existing without water in the stationery cupboard. Could still be now."

"Yes, that's true." The Captain looked puzzled for a few seconds. But then, a thought came to him. "It might be that they need to live in water until they grow a little. They need water to be nurtured and then once grown, they can survive for a time without it."

"Makes sense. So the one in the Train is fully grown."

"No idea. But it's definitely bigger than all these."

Paulo frowned. "All these? All what? There's nothing here. Where are they?"

The Captain returned his gaze to the pool beneath them, (and then so did Paulo). "You're looking at them."

Paulo got a rush of butterflies as he digested what the Captain had said. He swallowed and instinctively stepped back from the pool. "You mean they're living in the swimming pool?"

"Not just in the pool. In all the puddles around the edge too. Everywhere. Soon, they're going to grow up to be big strong . . . *whatevers*." The Captain grew frustrated at the fact that he still did not know exactly what these creatures were—what they were called—where they were from.

"Then they'll be *real* dangerous!" said Paulo.

"They're dangerous now. Probably more so, because we can't see them. We can't let them spread anymore. Remember what we found out about them. They probably reproduce by binary fission. They just divide and multiply. They'll multiply and multiply and multiply until they're all over the Earth."

"But if they rely on water to survive they won't be able to get far. I mean, how many places have a good body of water like this?"

"Paulo, you don't yet understand this planet. Earth is famous for its global water coverage."

"Can't be *that* much water sitting on the planet all at once."

The Captain put a hand on Paulo's shoulder. "Serothia might be a dry place, but what do you think covers about seventy percent of the Earth's surface?"

Paulo gulped in shock. "Not water?"

"Spot on pal! Paulo Vistar moves on to our special bonus round where he could win a luxury round-the-world cruise and . . . and we could drain the pool!!! Obvious solution. Where's Miss Reynolds?"

"I'm here," said Beth, re-entering the swimming pool room from her deed. "What's the prob?"

"We need to drain this pool, get rid of any trace of water. Can you make that happen?"

"Yeah but . . . what a waste. We've been on water restrictions, you know."

"Miss Reynolds, this is life and death."

"Fair enough."

"Couldn't you use it all on the lawn of the oval or something? I know about water restrictions. We have them all the time on Serothia." said Paulo.

"It's got chlorine and other chemicals in it. We normally would, but you have to wait days until all the chemicals disappear out of the water. So, it'll have to go down the drain."

Beth didn't ask any more questions, she just got straight onto the job. She located the drain line which she knew was in the filter pump near the pump motor. She went to a big storage cupboard, carried out a hose, attached one end to the drain line and carried the other end outside and led it to the drain near the road.

"Right, done," she said, walking back into the gym and brushing her hands together. "Anything else you need?"

"Anywhere else in the school where there'd be water lying around?"

"Er, toilets obviously. Running water is always available from any of the taps of course."

"Right, can we turn off the water supply altogether?"

"I think so. I should be able to work out how to do it."

"I'll know," said Paulo. "I did a bit of plumbing training at the Satellite Training Base. Just show me where it all is."

"Easy," said Beth. "Follow me."

They went out, leaving the Captain in the swimming pool room with Detective John Quest and a slowly emptying pool.

The detective put his hands in his pocket and strode smoothly over to the Captain, being careful not to step in any of the puddles. "So," he said, rather theatrically. "Taking the law into your own hands, are you?"

The Captain paused for a moment . . . and if you were there to see his face, you would have seen a slight smile appear somewhere on his mouth. "It's not as bad as pretending to *be* the law. I have always thought that it's a crime. So I will ask you once again . . . Who are you *really*?"

There was a pause before the detective replied. "Why are you so convinced that I am a fraud?"

"Okay, one: you call yourself Detective John Quest. Detectives aren't just detectives, they're detective sergeant, or detective constable. The way you're behaving, I would guess you're supposed to be a detective inspector or superintendent. But no, you're just 'detective'—very story-book. Two: you're alone. Usually detective inspectors or detective superintendents will have a sergeant or constables with them to do the dirty jobs, get down statements—that sort of thing. And three: you didn't show us a badge, and that's what policemen always do."

"I showed you a badge."

"You didn't give us a chance to see it properly."

"But I've got one."

"Let's have a look then."

Detective Quest didn't like this. The Captain, no matter what he did, always seemed to be in control of the situation. The detective knew that it was meant to be the other way around. Nevertheless, he took out his identification wallet again and handed it to the Captain.

"Gibberish," said the Captain, giving it a glance and then handing it back again. Then he stepped up and stood right in front of the detective so their faces were very close. "That *proves* it. So come on then . . . who are you really?"

The Captain shouldn't have stood so close to the man. Because from there, he could not see the man's hands, and right at that moment, the man raised his hands in a flash and clamped them tightly around the Captain's throat.

The Captain flung his own hands up to his throat to try and pull the detective's hands away. But the detective was very strong and the Captain found himself gasping for breath as his throat was being squashed shut. His second plan to defend himself was to just walk backwards away from his attacker, hoping that any second he would lose grip and the Captain would have a few seconds to arm himself with . . . a boogie board or part of a hose. But the detective did not lose his grip. He hung on just as tight—if not, tighter! The only thing the Captain was doing was backing himself into a corner from which there is often no escape.

The detective (or as we should now call him 'the man' as we now know he was not a real detective) had the Captain pinned to the wall. The Captain tried everything to get out of his hold. He twisted and jerked his body. He flailed his legs around to try and kick the man but nothing worked. Quest seemed to have the strength of ten and within seconds, the Captain was sure the hands would crush his trachea completely and he would be dead!

The man started saying, "You will *not* interfere," over and over as the Captain gasped and gulped and heaved and coughed.

Just when the Captain's lungs were almost completely empty and couldn't last any longer with no air getting to them, Beth walked in with Paulo saying, "Okay, we've turned off all the . . . CAPTAIN!!!"

The two of them rushed in and attacked John Quest from behind beating his back and pulling him away from the Captain. They were not successful in this particular job, but their presence was enough to distract him and he released the Captain ever so slightly to see whether he could get rid of the annoying prodding he was feeling in his back.

This was enough for the Captain to break free entirely, but now Quest was advancing on Beth and Paulo instead, raising his arm—about to knock them down with a terrible, fatal blow. The Captain grabbed the arm and struggled with it in order to give Beth and Paulo time to get out of the way. With his other hand, the Captain reached around the man's face, grabbed hold of . . . something, and the most extraordinary thing happened. With an elaborate gesture, the Captain pulled his arm back, ripping off some fleshy, rubbery object from the man's face. In fact, it *was* the man's face. And now, there were metal parts, running motors and little lights flickering on and off where his face should have been. However, this did not slow him down or distract him in any way, so while the Captain was in an advantageous position, he reached one hand into the metallic maze of a face, pulled out some wires and Detective John Quest ceased to move. The lights went off, the motors stopped running. Detective John Quest appeared to have been switched off.

"What on Serothia is going on?" said Paulo after a long moment of silence while everyone was staring at the broken man.

"Android," said the Captain, confidently. "I suspected as much as soon as I heard him talk."

"Why doesn't that surprise me?" said Beth.

"Well I would never have guessed. Why was he strangling you?"

"He's got one purpose, and it's probably to do with our pest problem. According to him, I was interfering so he did what he had to do. Probably what he was programmed to do."

". . . Programmed by whom?" Paulo said.

The Captain looked at him with just his eyes. "I don't know."

"Well it's simple isn't it," said Beth.

The Captain and Paulo both looked at her, questioningly.

She paused, just looking at them for a while without speaking. Then, after a short silence, said, "Oh you're ready to listen now? . . . Okay, well . . . it's a spaceship. On the other side of the oval, tucked away in the bushes. Looks like it crash-landed."

Chapter Thirteen

Invasion

Evelyn was just so puzzled. She couldn't fathom why that little, innocent, normal, young girl would be sitting deadly still on the edge of the sickroom bed, staring into a bucket of water. It was starting to worry her. She didn't know why, but there was just something so eerie about it. She knew Ruby wasn't herself, and she had seen people 'influenced' by alien intelligences before, but this was particularly spooky—probably because of the very fact that it was just a sweet, innocent seven year old. She sat there so still, but with a fire in her eyes as if on the inside, she was bubbling with angry, urgent anticipation. It was like at any moment, she could lash out and do something crazy like tip the water on herself or splash it all around the room or start kicking the walls.

In the next moment, Ruby stood up, gently placed the bucket on the floor in the middle of the room and calmly walked to the big window that Evie was looking through. Evie reflexively got up and backed away a little bit, heart beginning to race . . .

And then Ruby did something crazy.

She picked up the chair that was next to the bed and threw it hard at the window. It shattered—an explosive sound out of all the quietness. Glass flew everywhere; Evie covered her face. Ruby was not phased, even though bits of glass where landing in her thin, white-blonde hair. She stepped up onto the bed, walked across it and stepped straight out of the window—heading for Evie, who was cowering against the wall.

She stood on the chair Evie had been sitting on so that she was the same height as her. Then she pinned Evie to the wall by pressing her hand around her neck. It was such a little hand, yet somehow Evie was perfectly immobilised.

Ruby then did an even crazier thing. She raised her free hand up to her mouth, licked her index finger, and while staring deeply into Evie's eyes, wiped her wet finger down Evie's cheek and whispered, "We. Must. Survive."

The clouds above were as black as the sky beyond them. A distant rumble of thunder could be heard as Beth led the Captain and Paulo across the school oval.

"It's just behind those bushes," Beth said as they approached the other side. As soon as she'd finally been able to tell the Captain about her little discovery, to say he was extremely interested, would be an embarrassing understatement.

"A spaceship, huh?" Paulo gulped.

"Convenient place to crash-land," said the Captain, thoughtfully "behind some bushes."

"I wonder how long it's been here," said Beth.

"Well, let's have a look at it," said the Captain, plunging past the bushes with bold strides.

It wasn't very big, and it looked like what could be called 'a flying saucer', (except it was not flying at this moment.) You could see dents and scratches in different areas of its hull, from its collisions with trees and rocks on its way down from the sky.

"It must have been sitting here ever since that little girl found the creature," said Paulo. "And even longer."

"Did you take a look inside, Miss Reynolds?"

"No. I wanted to tell you about it first."

"This looks like the hatch operator," the Captain said, reaching for some buttons which were on the side of the ship.

"Do you think that's a good idea?" asked Paulo.

The Captain pushed the button he guessed was the 'open' one, and they discovered that the crash had not affected the mechanics of the doorway. But it slid open with a jerky, scrapey wheeze.

"It's not very big. Will we all fit in there?" asked Paulo.

"We're certainly going to have to crouch," said the Captain beginning to crawl inside.

The opening was dark, but not completely dark. The explorers could see a glow of light coming from further inside the vessel, which lighted their way.

Beth went to step in after him and suddenly, her face changed and she froze solid, feeling a bit sick. She drew in a sharp breath and swallowed. *She had felt something long and cold and limp flop across her foot.* She dared to peer downwards with just her eyes—as her head was almost paralyzed. "Captain," she squeaked timidly.

They all stood still and looked down slowly at Beth's foot. Draped across it, was a long, grayish, freckly arm. Hand on one end, palm facing upwards, and at the other end supposedly a body, but it was unseen. The arm was protruding from a little opening to the side of the outer door the Captain had just stepped through.

The Captain turned carefully and crouched down from where he was up in the entrance of the space craft. The opening was a half opened electronic door, and again the Captain found the controls to it. When the door slid completely open, they saw the rest of the alien body that looked like it had been dead for quite a while.

The Captain was about to squat down and lift the arm from Beth's foot, assuming Beth wouldn't want to touch such a thing. But he was wrong; Beth had already started bending over herself to lift the arm carefully off her and she stayed kneeling by the entrance of the ship to observe the strange skin of the alien.

The inner door the Captain had just opened lead into what looked like the control centre of the space ship, and the alien was lying across its floor, one arm hanging out of the door, and the other, clutching a communications device which was connected to the control deck. It was a small thing. Probably about the size of a twelve year old boy, but skinny and bald. It was wearing an all-in-one beige-coloured jumpsuit thing with a zip in the front, no sleeves. Its eyes were closed, and its small pursed mouth was completely colourless.

The Captain crept inside, having to stoop to fit his head in, and when he stepped over the unfortunate creature, he noticed straight away that there was another one further in, also dead, in a chair facing the control deck. He immediately observed all the technology in that room—no lights on or mechanisms humming—much of the control panel looked damaged and beyond repair.

He tried pressing a few buttons* but nothing worked. Everything was completely dead.

"I wonder what happened," the Captain thought out loud.

"Captain," said Paulo, pointing in from outside, "there's a little light on. Down there."

The Captain found the light and discovered it was part of the communication mechanism. He knelt down and took the little metal microphone device from the first alien's hand. He flicked some switches on and off and started speaking into the transmitter. "Hello, this is . . ." he found a name printed on the control panel, "OM93 . . ." and then there were some strange foreign words he did not recognise, so he just omitted them from the transmission. "Do you read me? This is Space Craft OM93, does anybody read me? The vessel has crash-landed on the planet Earth . . ." then he hesitated, and regretted to say, ". . . no survivors." He waited for a reply. There was none. "We'll try again in a minute, but I don't think the communication link was intended to reach this far."

"You don't think they intended on coming to Earth."

"It's just a guess so far."

"Captain," said Beth. "How do you know there *weren't* any survivors?"

"I suppose we don't know for sure, but the size of the ship gives us a clue."

"They're not very big," Paulo pointed out.

---

* Having seen many different kinds of spaceships and alien technology in his time, he always knew what kind of buttons to press to test them and try to get them working.

"OM," the Captain said thoughtfully to himself. "OM93. Can you see any other writing anywhere which might give us a clue as to where these guys came from?"

Beth stepped up into the room to look around, bending over at the hips so she could fit. Paulo came closer, but the three of them couldn't all fit in at once. "Um . . . here's OM93 written again over here, but nothing else."

"The navigation systems have packed up," said the Captain. "So I can't tell what their route was or their destination. No hand-drawn charts anywhere?"

Beth shook her head, while Paulo decided to step up into the space ship too. He passed the opening where the aliens, Beth and the Captain were and proceeded on through to the other section of the craft.

There was dim, buzzing, flickering light straight ahead of the tiny eerie passageway, and when he reached the end (which was no more than three small steps), he came to a little, round room. And on the curved walls around him, were lots and lots of slim, flat, glass containers. They were stacked high on top of each other on shelves that were secured to the wall with clamps and bolts. All except one section of the room. There was one panel of shelving that had broken away from the wall and as a result, the slim glass containers had slid off the shelves and nine or ten of them had smashed and lay in shattered pieces all over the floor. Paulo frowned in thought, trying to figure out what it could mean. When he stepped closer to a shelf of in-tact glass containers, he noticed a little label above the stacks.

"Eureka," said the Captain.

"What?"

"Look. A screen that isn't smashed." He fiddled with some wires behind the screen and pressed some more buttons and . . . "Voila!"

"It's working!" Beth exclaimed. "Is it still programmed. Does it say whether they were on a mission? Does it have on there what their mission was?"

"Hang on, patience, patience. Slow down baby, now you're movin' way too fast!"

"Sorry? Oh, I get it. It's the Beatles again."

The Captain looked at Beth, for a tiny second, confused. Then he remembered.

"I know all about your favourite band."

This was a little unnerving for the Captain. Just how much did this lady know about him?

"I suppose you know my favourite colour."

"Green."

"My favourite animal?"

"Lion. But your father didn't let you have one when you were six."

"My father's name?"

"Reginald."

". . . My birthday?"

"Third of November 18 . . . 97. Or 96? Sorry, can never remember which." Beth smiled kindly and met the Captain's gaze when he looked at her.

He narrowed his eyes slightly.

"Come on, this must happen all the time surely," she said, lightening the mood. "You meeting someone who's already met you or visa-versa. Things rarely occur in chronological order. Just never mind about me, the last thing I want to do is freak you out, and er . . . something's come up on the screen behind you."

"Ah good! There's life in the old thing yet. Now, let me see . . ." All the language on the screen was foreign, but this was no barrier. The Captain pulled out a little black box from his pocket. He pressed a tiny button on it and placed it next to the computer and a little blue light on it flashed on and off.

"Is that the Vernacular Recognition and Decoding Box?"

"Yes, no doubt you've seen it and probably used it before."

"I have, but not like that."

The Captain looked pleasantly surprised, and he took the liberty to explain to her. "Well, there's a clever little thing that I put inside it which makes it connect wirelessly to any computer. The box is usually for translating spoken language, but I've made it so that it can talk to the computer and decode the inbuilt programmed language."

"Inspector Gadget, eat your heart out."

"Here we go, details on the OM93. It's a mission alright. OM93 is the name of the ship . . ."

"Yes, we know that. But what does OM stand for?"

The Captain was searching for and reading information as he found it. ". . . Omran Space Mission . . ."

"What was the mission?"

". . . A global appeal for the Omran Bother Management Mission."

They were confused.

"Bother Management Mission? What's that supposed to mean?"

"They're from Omrah," said the Captain, in a whispered realisation—more so to himself than to Beth.

"From where?"

"A planet called Omrah. You haven't heard of it? Oh. Well, these," he indicated toward the dead pilots. "are Omrans and they've come from Omrah—a planet quite close, in fact I think it's in a neighbouring solar system."

Beth couldn't help laughing. "Omrah? Omrans from Omrah? Well . . . what does *bother management* mean?"

"Well it's obvious isn't it?"

". . . Well . . . maybe to some people."

"We're only relying on a computer generated translation. Words here and there are only an estimation of what it means."

She wasn't quite understanding yet.

"Come on . . . *Bother Management.* Another word for bother."

"Annoy?"

"Not a verb. Noun noun."

"Er . . . annoy*ance*, nuisance, pest . . ."

"PEST!!! Come on, use your head. Another word for management . . ."

". . . Pest . . . Manag . . . Control?" She gasped, "Pest Control Mission!"

"Exactly!"

"Captain!" called a voice from a little way away.

"Sounds like Paulo," said the Captain.

"Where is he?"

They found him in the inner room of the Omran space ship.

"Look at this," Paulo said when they reached him. It was evident he was still a little confused.

But when the Captain stepped inside the round room, everything finally made sense to him. "And here they are. All caged up," he said.

"What?" said Paulo.

"The pests."

"Not all of them," said Beth, pointing to the broken glass.

"That explains how they got loose here in the school." The Captain, stooped over, walked across to one of the shelves with the flat glass containers all stacked on top of each other. He looked at the label underneath. "They appear to be called Kratnids." Then he looked closely at one of the containers—saw nothing. He took out his Miniature Portable Microscope and peered through the lens and sure enough, there were hundreds of tiny living things all wriggling and skittering around inside just one of those small containers.

Paulo suddenly stepped well away from the broken glass on the floor. "There must be thousands of them around here—loose! We'll all be at risk of getting infected!"

"Relax Paulo," the Captain said, and then checked around on the floor with his microscope to make sure. "They've all scurried away in search of water to survive, most probably. The dangerous places are where there's water. Mainly the school swimming pool."

He put his microscope away and stood up straight.* "From what I understand the Omrans were having a major pest problem on their planet. It must have been pretty crucial for them to plan a mission to capture them all (don't know how they would have accomplished that, but they did), store them aboard this ship and dispose of them in the silent no-man's land called Outer Space. Their ship went off course, they ended up in the

---

* Well, as straight as he could without bumping his head on the ceiling.

Earth's gravitational pull and then wallop. *We're going to Australia!!** called the little green men from Omrah."

"They looked more sort of grey," said Paulo.

The Captain said from the corner of his mouth, "Another one of those expressions, Paulo."

"So now we've got their pest problem," said Beth. "The Invasion Of The Kratnids," she said, rather dramatically.

The thunder rumbled again, only this time, the sound was a little nearer, and the clouds above, were growing denser by the minute.

Evie had felt an odd feeling on her face shortly after Ruby had done that strange thing, and so she rushed to find a mirror. She found one in the staff toilet and was horrified at what stared back at her. A white spot, which had never been there before, was erupting on her left cheek. She caressed it with her finger and a look of absolute dread filled her eyes. Ruby was next to her, staring up into the mirror also.

Within seconds, a second spot crept onto the surface of her forehead.

"It is us," said Ruby to Evie's reflection. "It is the Kratnids. We are only trying to survive. If you fight us, we'll fight you and eventually kill you—like that foolish man."

Evie was panicking, as she watched another spot appear near the first one, while the other ones grew.

---

* He yelled this out loud with his arms in the air, in a deep voice and American accent. It was around this time that the famous Oprah Winfrey made her big famous trip to Australia and he was finding the similarity between the names amusing.

"But if you let us in, we'll protect you. We'll keep you alive."

"Yeah so you can use me like you're using her. It's wrong, you can't use human bodies like that!"

"We can. You're already doing it," said Ruby, as though she was no longer talking to Evie, but to a fellow Kratnid standing there."

"I can't! I can't!" More spots were popping up slowly, becoming part of her skin. And spots were growing on top of the existing spots.

"You can. Just let go. You don't have to die. You can live and those ugly white spots will go away. Just allow us in!"

"I can't! No! It's horrible!" Evie was struggling so much in her mind. She was fighting to keep control of it, but with every second, she could feel parts of it were being torn away like the strong ocean currents inevitably tear away the foundations of a sand castle. She was fighting a losing battle. "I c-c-can't!" She began to cry out loud. "No! Ruby, you've got to fight it too, Rrrruuby!" Evie had her head in her hands, feeling as though she could rip her hair out.

Ruby shook her head slowly. But it wasn't Ruby really, was it?

Evie gasped for breath, and after that, she breathed slowly in and out to try and gain some control over herself, but soon, she started closing her eyes, and a couple of those white spots started to wane.

Chapter Fourteen

Deadly H²O

"If we don't do something about this now, this world could be at war," said Paulo.

"It won't be a war, Paulo. Seventy percent water . . . it'll be a clean take over."

"No pun intended with the *clean*," said Beth, grimly.

"You're right, that wasn't intended. Sorry."

"But for what purpose?"

"No purpose really. They just want to survive. And who can blame them?"

The three of them were now standing outside the Omran ship.✢

"If they can only survive through water, the simple solution is we all stay dry," said Paulo.

"Slight problem there Paulo. Roughly sixty percent of our bodies are made up of water. Seventy percent of the brain is water. How is the whole human race going to stay dry if they themselves need water to survive?"

"Right, got the point."

✢   Because I can guess that their backs had started aching considerably.

While they were talking, out of the darkness behind them, came a slow, lumbering, faceless figure.

"Captain! Watch out!" Paulo yelled.

He whizzed around and just caught the heavy arm of the android/detective before it could come powering down on the Captain's head which would surely have knocked him out cold.

While it was struggling with the Captain yet again, Paulo and Beth scurried around to try and attack it from behind. Beth found a thick fallen branch from the surrounding trees. Paulo found some debris from inside the crashed spaceship and they were about to strike, when the Captain shouted, "Wait! Don't!"

"He'll kill you!" cried Beth.

"No no! I mean, yes he will, but before he does, we could talk to him!"

The android seemed to realise they were talking about him. Its circuits were damaged, so he was even dottier than before, but he understood what was being said.

"What could could we have to to talk about?"

"Isn't it obvious? The Kratnids!" he said with a wide grin.

"You know of the Krat Krat . . . . nids?"

"We do now. We know everything. And let me guess, you were sent by the Omrans to explore what had gone wrong with the mission. Right?"

Paulo and Beth started to lower their weapons. The android seemed to have been successfully distracted from his mission to kill.

"I'm afraid that's police business, not-not yours. You all st-st-still have to come with me so I can get down some official st-st-statements."

"Your cover's blown now, you don't need to pretend you're a policeman anymore. So . . . am I right?"

He straightened up. "Affirmative. I am a Questing Android, model TS54. Directive: to seek out obstacle preventing missi-mission accomplishment-shment and rectify. Report back. Then request recall."

"So how did you get here? You must have a little capsule too."

"Negative. I was teleported."

"Ah. Well, you would have a communication link with Omrah!"

The android paused. There was a soft robotic humming and ticking noise from within him. Then he replied, "Communication systems damaged. Unable to establish link."

"Oh great," said Beth. "I think we have you to thank for that, Captain."

"Yes alright, how was I to know?"

"You pose a threat to my mission Mr Captain and company," said the android. "My orders were to dest-dest-destroy any threatsss."

"No no no no no, wait, wait! We probably want the same thing, you and I. You want to stop the spread of the Kratnids, don't you?"

"Affirmative."

"You want to capture the ones that have got loose and any extra ones that have been created during their time here and send them off into deep space, do you not?"

"Affirmative."

"Well snap! Because that's what I want to do. And . . . company," he pointed to Beth and Paulo. "The Kratnids have already killed one Earth person, and taken over the mind of another and we don't want it to go any further."

"My concerns are not with this planet."

"I understand that, but in rectifying one problem, i.e. getting the Kratnids back into their cages, we rectify the other problem automatically, don't we. Savvy?"

The gentle robotic humming started again and after a few seconds, the android answered, "Affirmative."

The Captain smiled and held out his hand for a hand shake. "Team?"

"Affirmative," he replied, taking the Captain's hand and shaking it as he'd been programmed to do, in case the situation was to arise.

"Okay, put this in your memory banks," said the Captain. "The reason the mission failed, is that the Omran travellers crash-landed here and I hate to tell you, but they're dead."

There was no emotional reaction in the android. The Captain didn't know why he expected one. After all, his face was a good 200 metres away in the room with the swimming pool.

He went on. "Some of the cages are smashed and that's how some of the Kratnids escaped. Can you repair the cages and is there any equipment on board this ship that is especially built for catching the little critters?"

"I will locate the required equipment," he said.

"Good! We can work it out and get it straight," he then looked at Paulo and Beth, seriously ". . . or say goodnight."

Just as he said the word 'night', the Captain felt a drop of rain pat down on his nose.

Paulo raised up his hand, palm facing the sky. "Captain, you know how you said wet places would be the most dangerous . . ."

"Yes," he said nervously, going cross-eyed to look at the drop of water on the tip of his nose. "John Quest, or whatever your name is, you know all those instructions I just gave you . . ."

"Affirmative."

"Can you carry them out really really fast? There's a good chap."

The Captain felt confident about leaving the Questing Android back at the spaceship, while he, Beth and Paulo ran back towards the staffroom. It was what he was created for—to help recapture the Kratnids and stop them from endangering people. So he had no doubt that the robot would not double cross them. He was just a little concerned about the pitter pattering of the rain as it was falling from the sky, getting heavier and heavier by the second!

"Where are we going now?" asked Paulo.

"To the staffroom again to see how Ruby's getting on. Whatever you do, *don't step in any puddles!* You don't know where the Kratnids might be!"

"Lucky the children aren't here," said Beth. "They can't resist puddles."

They stepped inside the staffroom where they had left Ruby in the sickroom, and Evie at the front desk minding her, and what they found was . . .

Ruby sitting on the bed in the sickroom, and Evie on the chair at the front desk minding her. Everything normal.

Excellent, thought the Captain. *I knew I could rely on Evelyn.* "Well, how's everything going in here?" he asked.

"Fine," Evie replied flatly. "Getting better all the time."

"What do you mean by that?"

"That should be *your* line, Captain," said Beth with a slight smile, referring to what Evie had said. "Your 'Beatle-mania' must have rubbed off onto your friend."

"Well Evelyn, I must say, you've done a smashing job. Is the patient any better? Or worse?"

Just as the Captain had said 'smashing', Paulo had walked further into the room and discovered something terrible.

"Er, Captain?"

"Yes?"

"Something's not right."

The Captain was usually very observant. But it was Paulo first, who sensed something was wrong. Of course, it wasn't just a feeling, it was the glass scattered everywhere beyond the sickroom wall that was the dead giveaway that something had gone awry.

"What's happened here?" the Captain asked Evie, worriedly.

Evie didn't reply.

The Captain went over to the broken window to check on Ruby, and then that's when Evie spoke up.

"Do not go near her. We must survive."

The Captain turned back to Evie again. She had no spots on her face anymore, not that the Captain, Beth and Paulo had seen any spots on her yet. But now that she had let the Kratnids use her, her body was not sick from them.

"Who must survive?" asked the Captain, knowing what the answer would be.

"The Kratnids. Steps have been taken." Evie stood up. "Despite your attempts to sabotage us, our survival is un-jeopardised. The water supply has been turned back on and the big water pit is refilling."

"Why do you need the swimming pool?" Paulo asked, "when there's a whole world of water out there on this planet?"

"I wasn't going to tell them that," the Captain mumbled out the corner of his mouth.

Evie replied: "In order to find big supplies of water, we need to be able to survive without it for varying periods of time. In order to do that, we need to grow and become strong. To grow, we need water. The water pit is the nearest supply. And the room in which it lies makes a perfect environment for nurturing and cultivating. A breeding ground for the Kratnids. Anymore questions?"

"I have a question," said Beth quietly, by the Captain's side. "Since when did the things have a language? How can they be talking to us?"

"Actually that's a good question," said the Captain, louder, so that the Kratnids inside Evie and Ruby could hear. "How come you can speak? The one we found in the cupboard didn't speak to us."

"That's a dumb question. Being in control of a human's mind doesn't just mean we control their body—voice box and all, it means we're inside their mind. I know all this human's thoughts, beliefs, memories, and knowledge—which includes knowledge of the English language."

"Oh yeah, should have thought of that. Pretty obvious now you've explained it. Thanks."

"Captain," Paulo whispered, "What are we going to do about Evie and Ruby?"

"Right yes, we should do something."

"But what?"

"I'm going to try and talk to Evie. I know she's in there somewhere."

Paulo had bad memories of another time recently, when Evie had lost control of her mind.[*] Paulo had tried talking to her on that occasion—and it had been an impossible task.

The Captain took a step towards her. "Evelyn, I know you're in there and I know you can hear me. I know it's hard my girl, but you've got to try and fight. Fight with all your strength. And if that doesn't do it, the Lord's strength certainly will. Come on Evie. Fight them!" He risked putting his hands on her shoulders and he shook her gently. Then a little bit harder. "Evie! Come on! You can do it!"

Suddenly, everyone in the room heard the sound of a car roaring and then skidding off down the road.

"Who's that?" The Captain said, spinning around. Paulo had been by his side trying to help Evie and so all he saw when he turned around was Ruby, smiling, drenched from head to toe—she'd been out in the rain.

"Where's Miss Reynolds?" he said angrily to Ruby, (or more accurately, to the Kratnids inside her.)

"I was going to use this bucket of water, but when there's such lovely weather outside, why play indoors?"

---

[*] This was when they were in The Sanctuary and instead of a water-absorbing mammal-insect, it was due to a patch on her arm which made her forget all her troubles so she wouldn't try to escape the prison she was in.

"What did you do to her?" asked Paulo, worriedly.

"I was only playing in the puddles." Ruby shrugged and smiled. "We needed someone who could drive."

All the creases in the Captain's face straightened out as he went pale and asked, "Drive where?"

Chapter Fifteen

Temporary Solutions

"Captain look!" It was Paulo's voice yelling out and he was pointing at Evie.

She was down on her hands and knees in what looked like pain, but when the Captain spun around to see, he knew it was not pain—but the battling for control over her own mind.

He dived down onto the floor next to her, cheering her on. Paulo noticed suddenly that there were white spots appearing on her face and it was this that encouraged the Captain to keep on encouraging her.

Paulo was anxious, "Captain, didn't that P.E. teacher die from those white spots?"

"He died of dehydration. The white spots are just a symptom. Come on Evie, you've got to fight!"

She yelled back with gusto, "I have fight . . . ted. I've fought! What else do I have to do?"

"Evie! You're back!"

"What happened? Did I do something terrible? How's Ruby? Where's Beth?" She was climbing back up onto her feet.

"Why weren't the white spots there before?" asked Paulo.

"I can only assume that when the Kratnids enter the body, they can either take over your mind and therefore use you for their survival, or just kill you by draining you of all your water. If your mind isn't strong enough to fight them, why would they kill you when they could survive through you? Feeling dry at all, Evie?"

She opened and shut her mouth. "I do kind of have a dry mouth . . . oh no. They're going to kill me aren't they? Like the P.E. teacher. He must have fought back and so they killed him!"

"Now, try not to panic, Evelyn," said the Captain, patting her on the shoulder, now also starting to feel concerned at what Ruby was doing. She was standing in the doorway of the front office watching and waiting for the arrival of a car.

"I tried to get Ruby to fight them, Captain," said Evie, "I really did! But the real Ruby just wouldn't come out."

"Or couldn't."

"Maybe little children are more susceptible," said Paulo.

"Hmm?"

"Well their minds wouldn't be very strong or determined. They wouldn't realise they have to fight for control. They'd let it happen much more easily. Maybe that's why Ruby's so hard to reach."

"Yes, but they've just overtaken Beth as well," said Evie.

Ruby then turned around, rolling her eyes as if she was in the company of very slow-thinking dumbos. "Yes, because we needed a car."

The Captain was trying to think why and where they would need to go. And suddenly, Paulo's words were resonating in his head. "The minds of little children, *of course!*" He turned to Evie and Paulo. "The Kratnids don't want to *go* anywhere, they're coming straight back here! *With lots of little children.* Am I right?!" he spun round and asked Ruby.

Ruby just continued watching the car park.

"Beth, being a teacher, would know where a lot of those children live. Especially her own class, which is about . . ."

"Thirty kids," said Evie.

"I think she's gone to get more victims. To make the Kratnids stronger and more in number."

"Could Beth do that?" asked Paulo.

"I don't see why not," said Evie. "She kidnapped me when she wanted to find the Captain. Besides, it isn't Beth anymore is it? It's the Kratnids inside her."

"Well why are we all standing around doing nothing?" said Paulo. "Shouldn't we be doing something?"

The Captain was trying to think. *What* can *we do?* When in doubt, the Captain would usually run to where the action was. *Where's the action?* "The swimming pool!" he said suddenly and led the others past Ruby and outside. "Hold it!!" he clamped his fingers onto the door frame to stop his body from powering forward from the momentum. Paulo collided into the back of him, and Evie collided into the back of Paulo. "The rain, the rain," the Captain exclaimed. "As long as it's raining, the Kratnids could theoretically be flying through the air."

"How do you Earth people stay dry when it's raining" Paulo asked Evie.

"Use an umbrella."

"What's an umbrella?"

"It's a sort of poppy-uppy thing, a big shelter you can carry around with you everywhere. It looks like a mushroom, kind of. But when it's not popped up it looks like a short fat plastic stick with silky material wrapped around it."

"Well thank you, Evelyn for that wonderful description of an umbrella," said the Captain, placing his hands on his hips, "But I don't think a description will do us any good out in the pouring rain."

"Oh yes it will!" said Paulo. "I saw a bunch of those in one of the drawers when we were having a shifty earlier!"

"Fantastic! Where?"

He tried a few different drawers, trying to remember which one it was, until he found them at last. The Captain just about dived in, pulling out three of them. "There you go. One for you, one for you and one for me. Let's go! But don't go near the puddles, whatever you do!!"

"Shouldn't someone stay and keep an eye on Ruby?" said Evie, feeling another spot popping up on the side of her nose.

"It's too dangerous. She'll be fine here by herself."

Ruby was still standing by herself, watching the car park, waiting.

So the three with umbrellas rushed across the small segment of the oval and came to the big gym building again, taking care not to get wet.

"What can we do here?" asked Evie when they had stumbled into the inner linoleum-floored entrance.

The Captain looked through the glass doors of the swimming pool room. "Yep, it's filling up again alright."

"I'll go and turn the water off again," said Paulo and ran back outside.

"Is it too dangerous to go in there, Captain?" said Evie, observing that looking through the door was as far as the Captain had got.

"Probably. But above that, it's locked. We can't get in to do anything."

"What exactly were you going to do anyway?"

He rubbed the back of his head as though he could feel a headache coming on. "I don't completely know. I'd probably do what Miss Reynolds did earlier and attach the hose to the drain line again, which you and Ruby must have undone before, but that's only a temporary solution."

Evie felt her face, and then opened and closed her mouth again. "I'm so thirsty! I need a drink."

"No. You can't drink. You'll only give them more strength."

"But I'll dehydrate!"

"You can drink water but they'll only drain it from you."

"It'll delay my dehydration won't it?"

"Yes," the Captain admitted, "but it's only temporary. Everything's just temporary!" He was starting to go mad with indecisiveness.

Paulo came rushing back in. "The system's jammed. I can't turn the water back off."

"Evie, what did you do?"

"I don't know. I can't remember a thing!"

Paulo could see the restless state they were both in. "What's the problem? I mean, I know what the problem is but . . . what is it?"

"Temporary solutions, Paulo. Things that don't last, we don't need them!"

"Well, all we need is a permanent solution," he said optimistically. "Let's think of one."

The Captain didn't reply. Nothing was coming to mind. In the swimming pool room, countless thousands of Kratnids were being born and nurtured, getting bigger and stronger. And draining the pool now would only spread them further anyway. On their way were child-sized walking Kratnid vessels, who would be able to stop the Captain and his crew from taking any action whatsoever. So he had to think fast and do something now, before they got here and prevented them. But what? What could kill the Kratnids? Water was supplying their life. What can kill water? *It's ridiculous*, the Captain thought. *There is no way to do this!*

Chapter Sixteen

Salt Of The Earth

"If you're right, Captain," Paulo was saying, "And Beth Reynolds is bringing more children here to infect, wouldn't it be better to wait for them and as they arrive, we could grab them and lock them up. They'll only be children, if your theory's correct. We can handle children."

The Captain thought about it for a moment. The little cogs and wheels in his brain were ticking wildly.* He looked at them and said, "Alright. We'll ambush them. We'll somehow hide around near the car park and when Miss Reynolds arrives with the children, we'll grab them. Hopefully they won't even be affected yet."

"Captain, aren't you forgetting about the rain?" said Evie. "Anything that's out in the open sky will get infected within minutes!"

"Keep up, Evelyn," said the Captain. "Listen."

She listened. They all did.

"It's stopped," she whispered.

"So we must take our chance while we have it."

"What about Beth though?" asked Evie.

---

* Figuratively speaking obviously, where as if it was the Questing Android, it would be literally speaking.

159

"Well I'm probably the strongest out of all of us. I'll grab Beth, you grab the children."

"Gently," said Evie.

"What?"

"Well they're only children."

"Evie, you can't restrain someone *gently*. But I see your point. Only use force if necessary. Like I said, the children might not even be affected yet."

"Right," said Paulo. "Then what?"

"Yeah well . . . I don't know after that. We'll see what the Kratnids have to say. As long as they don't get to use those children. And *we* have the power, right?"

"Right," they replied in unison.

Feeling confident, because they had a plan finally, they turned around boldly. Leaving their umbrellas behind, they opened the gym building door and bolted outside . . .

. . . Colliding with the sight of a young woman—Beth, and about seven little children around her walking slowly and calmly towards the building. Ruby was among them. The three nearly tripped over themselves from stopping so abruptly, and they had to hang on to each other to stop from stumbling to the ground.

"What's plan B?" asked Paulo.

The two groups were silently staring at each other for a few seconds.

"Miss Reynolds!" called the Captain.

She stopped, and the children stopped too.

"Listen to me, Beth, I know you're in there somewhere. You can fight the Kratnids. I'm sure you're strong enough!"

"Your words are useless, Captain," said the Kratnids, through Beth's lips.

Ruby started walking over towards the Captain, Evie and Paulo. But it wasn't them she was heading for.

Evie noticed the other children around Beth whispering to each other and looking confusedly up to their teacher.

Evie then whispered to the Captain. "I don't think they're infected yet."

He replied ever-so-softly to the both of them, "When Beth let's her guard down, get all the children somewhere safe, alright?"

They nodded their heads, but almost without any movement at all.

"I'm not talking to the Kratnids," the Captain then said out loud to Beth. "I'm talking to Beth Reynolds! Miss Reynolds, can you hear me? If you can, try and think of something. Something real and about you! Think of your mum and dad. Think of what you saw on television last night! Try and say something! Say some ultimately boring fact in maths that you teach your class everyday! Say something that's unique to Beth Reynolds, I don't know. Say something that's really uniquely Aussie . . ."

With this, Beth merely smiled slyly at her comrade, Ruby and said out loud to her, pointing to the children around her, "They're goin' *straight* to the pool room!"

And with that, Ruby ran to the half a dozen children and tried to get them to follow her.

"Why should we go anywhere with you, *teacher's pet?*" asked one of the boys.

"Yeah, what's going on? Miss Reynolds wouldn't tell us."

"Just trust me. Why don't we play *Follow The Leader* like we do at lunch time."

"But this is weird, being at school at night. Why are we here?"

"Just do as I say or . . . or I'll lick you!"

"What? That's yuck!"

"Well, I'll do it!"

"Oohhhh, I'm scared . . ." one said sarcastically.

Evie couldn't let her lick them. It sounds silly I know, but that was how Evie lost control of *her* mind to the Kratnids.

"Well," continued Ruby, talking to the children. "Do you want to play puddles with me?"

"Okay!" they all yelled, suddenly extremely happy to have Ruby as a friend, and now Evie *knew* she had to intervene. When she approached, Ruby threatened to harm her. But she thought to herself, *I'm stronger than a seven year old,* so she went to grab Ruby, pick her up, lock her in some room again—with no big glass windows. But when she did, Ruby fought back with an unnatural strength, and the next thing Evie knew, she was on her back on the hard paved ground in quite a lot of pain. And there, on the ground, for some reason, Ruby's words, 'follow the leader' resonated in her head. She'd heard the name of that game used by a man on Serothia, who had led her into a dark room and imprisoned her there.*

Back to the Captain. He started trying a different tactic with Beth. Rather than trying to talk to *her*, he decided to talk to the Kratnids.

---

* He was following orders at the time of a big blobby blue alien called an Ogrimite who had brainwashed him. For the record, the Ogrimites have no connection with the Kratnids.

"Look, Miss Reynolds is of no more use to you. You've already used her to bring the children here. Now let her go."

"We are about to go and get another load of children."

At this point, Paulo parted from the Captain's side and disappeared, unnoticed by anybody, including the Captain.

The Kratnids continued, "So you see Captain, we are not yet finished with Miss Beth Reynolds. We must survive."

She turned and headed to where her car was. The Captain knew he could not let her go again. This had to be stopped. "Evelyn! Don't let those children get into the pool room!" he shouted behind him and he was off.

But what the Captain didn't know was that Evie was temporarily incapacitated.* She could do nothing—only watch Ruby take those children wherever she wanted them to go.

The Captain was charging ahead to stop Beth—tackle her to the ground if necessary. By the time he reached the car park, however, she was already in the driver's seat of her car—she'd had a good head start. She turned the key in the ignition . . .

But the engine wouldn't start. The Captain was ready to hop into the passenger's seat to snatch the keys off her. But the engine wasn't starting. The Captain was amazed and puzzled and bedazzled and lots of words with 'z's in them, but Paulo was not so surprised. He emerged at that

---

* which is a big word which I am aware sounds like she'd lost her head, but it just meant that she was injured and out of action for a little while.

moment from behind some bushes near the car park, holding a piece of engine he had stolen from her car.

Their smiles at each other grew and grew. "Ignition coil lead!" Paulo called to the Captain. "I learnt how to disconnect one on Serothia. Did you know, the cars here on Earth are surprisingly similar?"

"Well done Paulo!"

While Paulo was enjoying his moment of success, Beth had gotten out of the car and was approaching him with fierce anger in her eyes. She had a huge folder in her hands—heavy with papers and other resources that she had found in the back seat of the car. She held it above her head and was about to swing it down hard on Paulo's head, but the Captain was there to stop her. He grabbed her arm tightly in his hand and the folder fell on the ground, the contents spreading everywhere. She struggled to break free of the Captain's strong grasp but had much difficulty. With Beth's attention now being fully on the Captain, Paulo had a chance to get away to try and help Evie who was still near the oval. The Captain was trying to drag Beth back towards the office building while she struggled with him. He didn't really know what he was going to do once he got her there, maybe lock her up in a room until he could think of SOMETHING PERMANENT.

Paulo had reached Evie and he tried to help her up. She cried out in pain though when she put weight on her right foot.

"I think I've sprained it. Don't touch me, you'll catch what I've got!"

"You might have just rolled it. Can you move your ankle around?"

The Captain and Beth were a little distance away, but the other two could still see them clearly from where they were on the edge of the oval, near the gym building.

"Paulo, leave me and make sure those kids don't get wet!"

"Right," he said, but something made him stop just as he was about to get up. Something he saw temporarily paralysed him. Evie saw it too. They were looking at Beth and the Captain and it was the 'totally unexpected' that happened. In fact, so unexpected that Evie and Paulo had to make sure their eyes weren't playing tricks on them or that they weren't too far away to see it clearly. Evie considered the possibility that the white spots had started growing over her eyes and affecting her sight.

But neither of these of course, were the case. They saw it clear as day. Even though it was night.

Beth had managed to pull free of the Captain's clutches with the strength that came from the Kratnids, only to grab hold of *him* this time and she locked him into a kiss. Evie and Paulo stared on, while the Captain seemed to have no strength whatsoever to pull away—and they could see that he was trying.

Evie then felt a little embarrassed. She felt like she shouldn't be looking. But Paulo frowned and kept on staring.

"What *is* going on?" he said.

"Is it any of our business?"

He had already started walking over, cautiously.

"Paulo!" Evie tried to get up. Once she'd managed that, she hobbled over to catch up to him.

"Oh no," said Paulo softly, almost under his breath.

"What?"

Finally, Beth released the Captain from her grip and once they were separated, she collapsed to the ground. The Captain, too, staggered back a little bit and he was now staring at his hands.

"The Kratnids obviously wanted the Captain," Paulo said to Evie. "And now they've got him." He ran over without hesitation.

"Wait Paulo! It might be dangerous!" She hopped, hobbled and limped after him and they could start to see, that on the Captain's hands were a few white spots. They grew bigger and spread fast, and when he looked up to face his friends, they were erupting all over his face as well.

He didn't say anything or do anything that made him look frightened. But Evie could see it in his eyes. It was how *she* felt inside as well.

"Egh, this feels horrible. Like having acne all over again."

"I know," said Evie.

"Hey look at us, we look like a pair of . . . a pair of . . ."

"A pair of people who are gunna die if they don't find a cure for Kratnid-infection any time soon?" cried Paulo.

"Yeah, something like that. Come on, I've got an idea."

They followed his wide, jogging strides over into the office building again.

"Will Beth be alright?" Evie asked, almost about to kneel down beside her.

"She's probably herself again, but leave her to gather her strength. Don't touch her Evelyn!"

"I wasn't going to."

"Come on. There's no time to lose!" Then he said more to himself, "Where's the kitchen in this place?"

He led Evie and Paulo into the staff kitchen, which he found just behind the front office and in the same room as the comfy couches and tables and chairs. He made a B-line for the kitchen cupboard-top and searched desperately all over it, until finally coming to the thing he was evidently looking for. It was a tall container of table salt and he immediately opened the lid and poured it all over himself, smearing it on his arms, gathering it in his hands and rubbing it into his light-brown, wavy hair. He then dug his face into his hands and gave himself a full, high-speed facial with the stuff. He even poured some into his mouth.

Beth walked in then and joined Paulo and Evie who were just standing there, staring at him with their mouths open. They didn't notice she was there until she spoke.

"What's he doing? Has he gone mad?"

They jumped a bit from her sudden presence and they knew straight away that she must have been free from the Kratnids. Just by looking at her eyes.

"Dunno," said Evie. "If he has gone mad, it's the Kratnids. But why isn't that happening to me?"

Paulo suddenly had a thought-wave. As though a little light bulb suddenly went on above his head. "Sodium chloride! Salt! It dries up stuff. Maybe the salt will dry up the moisture the Kratnids are using to take over his body."

Suddenly, the Captain had stopped his salt dance, slammed the half-empty container down on the cupboard top and demanded of his companions, pointing to himself, "Any dots? Any dots?"

In delighted and astonished realisation, the three stood before him, shaking their heads.

The Captain then replied as calmly as ever, "Good good good."

There was a long silence while the Captain tried to get salt out of his eyes, before Beth asked, "What happened?"

"In an attempt to further strengthen the Kratnid army and have control over my body as well as yours, they thought it'd be a good idea for you to kiss me so they could travel through the saliva, so that we'd both be infected."

"Yuck!" exclaimed Evie.

Beth's eyes widened and she suddenly went red. "So . . ." she cleared her throat, "how come I'm not infected anymore?"

"My only guess is that I drink more water than you so they favoured my body over yours."

"I drink *plenty* of water . . . some days."

"There you are. Because I'm in a perfect state of hydration, they hopped completely over to me rather than just a little bit. Understand?"

"I suppose."

"So where are they now?" asked Evie.

"Dead," the Captain replied in a somewhat indecisive way. He was happy to be free of them and not at risk of dying himself, but he never really *enjoyed* killing living things of any description. But, they were pests after all.

"But all the water in your body can't possibly be dried up, otherwise *you'd* be dead," said Paulo, a bit confused.

"You're right there. Keep an eye on my skin for anymore trace of the Kratnids. As far as I can tell though, they're gone, which tells us that the properties of salt aren't just drying to them but lethal as well. Handy for us, eh?"

"So, we finally have a way to control them?" asked Evie, excitedly. "A permanent one?"

"Looks like we might have. We'd better see what's happening in the swimming pool, don't you think?" He picked up the salt container again and tossed it to Evie. "Here, this is your cure by the way. Get stuck in."

Once again, the four of them came to the gym building and blasted through the doors with no fear.* The only child in there however, was Ruby—on her own, with the swimming pool still filling up, nearing the top.

"Where are the children?" the Captain demanded.

"Once we started playing in the puddles and in the swimming pool, they soon came around to my way of thinking—as you can imagine—and so then I sent them on useful errands around the school."

"Like what?" asked Beth.

"This and that. Turning on taps. In the yards, the bathrooms. Everywhere. There'll be Kratnids surrounding us like the hills surround this tiny city. But *this* is where they grow up and become strong," Ruby finished with a smile and at that moment, something grey and furry started crawling out of the swimming pool.

It was a Kratnid—like the one that was probably dead by now in the Train, but bigger. The Captain, Evie, Paulo and Beth backed away slowly as it crawled slowly towards them, gnashing its teeth and making horrible noises with every step. Then another one popped its head

---

* The doors were unlocked now obviously, because Ruby had taken the children through.

up above the water and crawled out. Then another one, and another one. Some bigger than others. The biggest, being about the size of a rolled up sleeping bag. They were walking, thriving mammal-insects that were multiplying by binary fission, and they were ready to take over the world.

Chapter Seventeen

The Fool In School Stays Mainly In The Pool

"The children are just a temporary solution, Captain," the Kratnids inside Ruby were saying. "Once the Kratnids have a foothold, they can grow bigger and more in number. As soon as this happens, when we're all big enough and strong enough, we won't need the children anymore."

"What does that mean?" asked the Captain. "That you'll dispose of them or that you'll release them and let them live?"

"Which one would you prefer?"

"Well the second one obviously," said Evie, then grimacing with the taste of salt in her mouth.

"They're only children," added Paulo.

"If our plan works and we survive on this planet, it seems rather pointless to keep them alive. They'll probably perish eventually along with all of you. Better sooner rather than later. Kratnids do not co-inhabit well."

This comment absolutely terrified Evie, Paulo and Beth. But the Captain was thinking more clearly. He whispered to his companions, "The Kratnids may be very determined and many in number, but they're not very smart. They're just instinctively trying to survive. Evie and Beth, I want you to try and get back to the staff room, avoid stepping in any puddles, and get more salt."

"There's not much left in that container."

"Then you'll have to find more. We're going to need it."

The two girls, having managed to sneak away when the Captain and Paulo distracted Ruby, rushed into the staffroom kitchen again and Evie went for the container of table salt.

"It's nearly empty!" she said, shaking it a little, listening to the grains—about three or four teaspoons—shiffering in the bottom.

"Tip it out into this, let's see how much there is," said Beth, pulling a plastic bowl out from one of the cupboards.

Evie emptied it out, making a tiny pile of salt in the bottom.

"That's not going to be enough. The Captain probably wants to use it to get rid of *all* the Kratnids. There's *heaps* of them now!"

"Well, maybe they only need a tiny grain to be killed by it."

"We can't be sure."

"Hang on, here's a salt shaker with a bit more in it," Beth said, picking it up and pouring the little bit into the bowl. "Well, *that* made a big difference," she said sarcastically.

"So, there's *no* more salt anywhere?" asked Evie, starting to feel worried.

Beth thought hard. "Hang on," she suddenly said, as though a light bulb had just flicked on above her head. "My left-over lunch is in the fridge, that'd be salty."

"What is it?"

Beth opened the refrigerator and pulled out a large microwave-safe bowl covered in cling wrap. She unwrapped it. "It's a Chinese-y, soy-saucy thing. Soy sauce is heaps salty!"

"Chuck it in!" Evie said with a big smile.

"Would that work?"

"The Captain just said he needs salt. We could chuck anything that's salty in here."

Beth poured it in. "Okay, what else have we got in here?" She scanned the contents of the fridge and the fridge door. She gasped. "You're not going to believe this."

"What?"

"There's a whole bottle of soy sauce here!" She picked it up. "That's right, Silvia had her spring rolls the other day. She must have brought this from home." Beth opened the cap and poured it in, saying, "Sorry Silvia. Your soy sauce is needed for a greater cause. Let's see, what else?"

Evie pulled out one of the utensil drawers and grabbed a large spoon and she started stirring the sloppy, salty concoction.

"Salad dressing! Full of salt!" Beth said, opened its cap and poured it in. Evie kept on stirring.

They laughed. "Ergh, yuck!"

"Margarine, let's see," Beth upturned the tub and looked at the ingredients. "Salt! The third ingredient listed, that's going in!"

"Wait, melt it in the microwave, it'll be easier to stir."

The girls made a great team.

Evie started looking in the cupboards right by her and listed what she found. "Packet soup, chocolate biscuits, yum. Canned soup . . ."

"Canned soup has lots of salt I think. Can opener." Beth proceeded to open the five large tins of soup and poured them in.

"You know this probably isn't very potent anymore," said Evie.

"Hopefully that doesn't matter. As long as we've got heaps of salt in there. Let me see, what else . . ."

"Oh my goodness! Potato chips! You've got potato chips in the cupboard!"

"Bung 'em in!"

"We're gunna need a bigger bowl."

While Evie transferred everything to a huge silver bowl she found, Beth was still darting round the kitchen in all the places she knew to look. "Soft drink, there'll be a bit in that. Oh! Jean's got pretzels stashed away in her drawer, here, catch!"

Evie mashed up the pretzels and the potato chips in the bowl.

"Anything else in those cupboards, Evie?"

"Er, tinned spaghetti, tomato sauce, barbecue sauce, cornflakes . . . cornflakes?"

"Lynette sometimes has her breakfast here in the mornings." Then Beth's eyes widened. "I'm pretty sure I read the other day that cornflakes have more salt in them than salted peanuts! Put them all in, they'd all have salt in them."

Evie did so, continuing to stir and looking in the cupboard. "Someone's beef jerky, yuck . . ."

"Great! Put it in!"

"Um . . . there's also . . . some salted peanuts in here."

Beth laughed. "Wow, God knew we were going to need all this salt didn't He? Either that or we teachers just eat an unhealthy amount of salt! Here, there was some of this stuff in the fridge too. Someone's left-over lunch—stir-fry by the looks. Smells like oyster sauce—probably salty." She tossed it to her. She gasped again. "I just realised where we'd find more salt too!"

"Where?"

"Judy would have some in her room. Her class is doing 'kitchen chemistry' in Design Technology. Salt is an essential ingredient for that. I'll be right back!"

While Evie stirred, Beth ran with a set of keys to the classroom next to her own. When she came back, she came back laughing—holding up what she had found.

"There's a whole bag!" And tipping it all in, she said, "I'll have to reimburse the Junior School budget for this."

The quickly growing Kratnids were getting closer and closer to the Captain and Paulo, forcing them back into the wall behind them. If they kept backing away, they would be trapped, and they wouldn't be able to duck past them in any way without being touched. There were five the size of a rolled up sleeping bag now, and the biggest one—the one right in front of them, was by now, approximately the size of a dining room chair. Suddenly, the boys felt the wall against their backs and they couldn't reverse any further. The Captain had a particularly lumpy part of the wall in the small of his back, and at a time like this, he wondered what it was. He risked a quick glance behind him and suddenly, he felt stupid, but grateful.

Without hesitating, he grabbed onto the lump with his right hand, pull down on it, grabbed Paulo's arm, and slid outside the door with him. He slammed the large glass door shut on the small hairy monster and flicked the little lock.

"First rule of escape," said the Captain. "Always have your back towards a door handle."

Paulo breathed a sigh of relief.

"That won't hold them for long."

"Can I be of any assis-sis-sistance?"

They turned around, and saw the Questing Android just in the main doorway of the gym, holding stacks of small, flat, glass containers.

"Oh, you've fixed the containers!" said the Captain, hustling them all outside into the open.

"I have fulfilled your orders. How will we trap them?"

The Captain breathed out a heavy puff of air and rested his hand on the android's shoulder. "That is a good question. Care to look in there? They are the pests we need to trap."

The android faced the doors and then faced the Captain again. (Except not having a face, he more sort of . . . *headed* him.) "Dilemma," he said calmly. "Pests are larger than the containers."

The Captain laughed. "Yes my friend. Well spotted. They've grown a little bit since you saw them last. So I'm afraid the trapping idea is off. But . . . seeing you again has given me an idea."

"Well it better be quick Captain because those glass doors aren't looking like much of a challenge for those things."

"Come on," said the Captain, "To the spaceship!"

The Captain was the first to reach the saucer-like spaceship and without hesitating, he hopped straight up into it, searching.

"What are you looking for?" Paulo asked when he arrived behind the Captain.

"A little room where the space suits are hanging. There's always a little room where the space suits are hanging."

"Well ask the android, he'll probably know."

The Questing Android was not far behind Paulo. His running certainly left a lot to be desired. The Captain asked him about the space suits and suddenly found himself hoping that Omrans *need* space suits to go out into space. They might be able to breathe when there's no air; they may not even breathe in the conventional way for all he knew.

Luckily, the Questing Android knew exactly what the Captain was talking about. "Through that hatchway, you should find some," he said. "All Omran spaceships are built the same."

They weren't hanging, because the space was too small, but they were folded neatly—two of them.

"Come on, Paulo," said the Captain enthusiastically, "try this on for size!"

"What? The helmet too?"

"Everything. Except we can't stop. We'll have to dress and run!"

"Where to?"

"To the staffroom!"

On opening the staffroom door, Paulo and the Captain heard loud, hysterical laughter, and occasional exclamations of "Ergh!" and "Yuck!"

"Don't spill it!"

"Don't worry, I won't," the girls were saying—still laughing.

"What's going on?" the Captain asked, finding Evie and Beth with red faces and a huge big bowl sitting on the floor, filled with soy sauce, salad dressing, margarine, canned soup, potato chips, soft drink, pretzels, tinned spaghetti, tomato sauce, barbecue sauce, stir-fry, beef jerky, salted peanuts, cornflakes, a Chinesy-soy-saucy-thing, and salt.

"Is this enough?" Evie said, grabbing the heavy bowl and walking up to the Captain. She and Beth sniffed and tried to be serious again."

"It'll have to be," said the Captain.

The girls started feeling worried.

The Captain read their expressions and decided to say with a little smile, "You've done a good job."

"It does look exceedingly yuck," said Paulo, gazing down into the lumpy, sloshy, salty mess

"Yeah well it's basically our life-line. Probably the world's life line. So let's get it over to the pool."

"Why are you wearing a space suit?" Evie said, suddenly thinking to ask. They were in the full suit, two or three sizes too small for them, but holding the helmets in their hands for now.

"Protection."

"What about us?" said Evie.

"You won't be getting that close."

Paulo started to worry. Just how close did the Captain have in mind?

"Come on, we have to go."

"We can't run though," said Evie, "otherwise we'll spill it."

They took it across the school yard, along the oval and towards the gym building nice and slow and steady. It was almost maddening, knowing the urgency of the situation and not being able to at least walk quickly. They could not afford to lose one drop. The Questing Android followed them wherever they went, walking along like an ordinary human being, but missing a face.

When they eventually reached the gym building, they saw that the double glass doors looked almost at breaking point now. Ruby was looking for a heavy object to smash the glass with.

"Okay, the plan," the Captain said while they were still a short distance from the entrance. "Paulo and I go in there and I tip this lot into the pool. Hopefully it'll be potent enough to contaminate the pool enough to . . ."

"Kill them?"

He nodded regretfully. "To kill them."

"And what can we do?" asked Evie.

"You two can keep trying to turn off the water supply again."

"Okay," both Evie and Beth answered and they started heading off.

"Oh and, stay away from the children," the Captain called after them.

"Children?"

"The ones infected by the Kratnids. They've scattered throughout the school."

"Oh. Righto," said Evie.

Evie had to explain about the children and how they came to be there, and Beth then felt terrible for having been responsible for putting seven of her students in terrible danger!

They left Paulo and the Captain standing outside the gym building, looking in.

"So," said Paulo, anxiously. "All the Kratnids in the pool will perish."

The Captain nodded.

"What about the Kratnids outside the pool?"

"Don't worry, I've got a plan for those too."

"That one at the door, it's huge! I'm sure it's grown more since."

"It has. They're not mammal-insects anymore. They're mammal-insect-monsters and if we don't get in there soon with this, they'll get bigger and stronger still and basically take over the planet. Not on purpose, they just want to survive . . . which makes what we're about to do, really morally hard."

"But it's for the greater good, Captain."

"The greater good for Humans, but not for Kratnids."

"But we're a higher life-form surely. It's right to save Humans from these pests isn't it?"

The Captain swallowed and then said, "Yes. God said we have authority over the fish in the sea and the birds in the sky and over every living creature that moves on the ground."

"That's all very well but how are we actually going to get in there? They're still hovering around the door and they'll stay there until they break through."

"Why do you think we're wearing spacesuits? You'll have to go in first and try and coax them away from the door so I can get in safely with this."

Paulo clicked his helmet on and the Captain picked up the bowl of soy sauce, salad dressing, margarine, canned soup, potato chips, soft drink, pretzels, tinned spaghetti, tomato sauce, barbecue sauce, stir-fry, beef jerky, salted peanuts, cornflakes, a Chinesy-soy-saucy-thing, and salt.

"I could tip this straight over them, but that won't do, it's only temporary. I need it in the pool. Got it?"

Paulo nodded. But then he realised his nod would not be seen from inside the helmet so he said out loud, "Yes."

"Got it?" the Captain repeated.

Paulo realised his voice could not be heard from inside the helmet, so he looked at the Captain, nodded and gave him the thumbs up—even though he didn't feel very brave and 'thumbs-uppy' at the moment. The Captain clicked on his helmet too and Paulo went forth.

His task was a scary one, but not all that hard. As soon as he managed to enter through a narrow gap in the door, the Kratnids seemed to lose all interest in the Captain and followed Paulo, thinking they were being given an easy feed. Paulo was an easy target, but what they didn't know, was that they wouldn't be able to find him in all that space suit.

The Captain easily got to the pool and he didn't hesitate to pour the salty concoction in. He saw grown (but small) Kratnids trying to climb out of the pool and tiny ones swimming around expertly and imagined how many more microscopic ones were in there absorbing the water like babies drinking milk. He watched the salty sludge swirl through the water, deeper and deeper, turning a small section of the pool a deep browny, purply colour . . . with lumps of potato chips and pretzels in it. He was hoping that the bowl of soy sauce, salad dressing, margarine, canned soup, potato chips, soft drink, pretzels, tinned spaghetti, tomato sauce, barbecue sauce, stir-fry, beef jerky, salted peanuts, cornflakes, a

Chinesy-soy-saucy-thing, and salt, added to the plain water in the pool would be strong enough.

There was a glimmer of hope when he saw one of the Kratnids which was climbing out of the pool, start to struggle and slow down. And then he suddenly felt a pounding of little fists on the side of his leg. Ruby had been sitting cross-legged on the tiled floor watching the ever-growing monsters with delight, but now she was at the Captain's side trying to stop him. He tried to control her but her little arms were unstoppable. He did not, however, feel the incredible strength that Ruby had apparently possessed before, and he wondered why. He saw that she had wet feet and supposed that some water from the pool had splashed up from the flapping, stringy, hairy arms of the Kratnids trying to get out. And it gave him a reminder of what he needed to do next. The first priority before anything else. Save Ruby.

He thought of picking her up and throwing her in the pool, but quickly stopped himself, saying, "Safety first," and he quickly scanned the room, found a roller-door and ran straight to it, feeling confident that Ruby would follow him wherever he went.

She did, and the storage area behind the roller door contained just what he wanted. He grabbed a small fluro-pink life-jacket and two foam noodles.* He thrust them into Ruby's hands and pulled the life-jacket down over her head, scooped her up in his arms and walked

---

* In case you're really confused, these are floating aids you can use to help you float in the swimming pool. If you are on an outing one day and happen to see some children, some parents and a swimming pool, you will more than likely see some of these.

down into the pool with her. She had no choice in the matter. She was helpless in his clutches. The water that had splashed onto her foot and ankle from the pool, had weakened the Kratnids inside her. And despite all her kicking and screaming, Ruby was fully immersed in the water. It was like a baptism, and when she came up again, her eyes had changed. She was still kicking and screaming, but it wasn't out of objection anymore, it was out of terror. And by looking at that change in her eyes, the Captain could tell that Evie and Beth's concoction had worked!

All Ruby could see now were big, little and in-between-sized monsters. Climbing out of the pool, struggling for life in the pool, and looming around near the pool. Also, she had an unidentified figure in a space suit holding onto her tightly. And to top it all off, she couldn't feel the bottom of the pool under her feet! The Captain lifted the terrified Ruby out of the water and plonked her down on the tiled floor. He then knelt down quickly in front of her and lifted his helmet up for a few seconds, saying, "It's just me. Remember me? You'll be safe now, don't worry."

"Safe? Are you sure?" All Ruby could see was a room full of monsters.

"You've got salt all over you," the Captain said, reassuringly. "If they touch you, they're dead. So if they know what's good for them, they won't come near you."

All Ruby could do was nod and let the Captain do what he needed to do.

Beth and Evie reached the place where the water supply for the school could be turned off. It was on the other side of the oval from the gym building in a fenced off area, and this time, with the strength of two people, the large tap moved with a rusty squeal, and the water was shut off. They immediately turned and started heading straight back across the oval, but were stopped abruptly by a little boy who had stepped out from around the corner of one of the buildings.

All he said was, "We must survive," and the girls knew they were in trouble. It was a narrow pathway beyond that building to get back onto the oval, and the boy was standing right in that pathway. Evie leant to one side, seeing if it was possible to duck past quickly, but the boy anticipated her movement, and reacted accordingly so she couldn't get past. Beth tried to duck around on his other side, but the boy stepped across, blocking her as well. He anticipated their every move and it was clear he was not going to let them pass. If they went for it, chances were one of them would be tagged by him. Beth thought how much like a game of Red Rover it was. Only this was not a game. The person who was 'it'—was literally poison.

Chapter Eighteen

Pest Control

The cure for any poison was the right antidote. They knew what it was of course, but they didn't have any on them at the moment. Evie thought back to when she was covered all over with the antidote. It was on her hands, in her hair, on her clothes, in her pockets . . .

While the child with a determined look in his eyes took another step towards them, (them feeling ridiculous, being terrified of a seven year old boy with his front teeth missing), Evie, filled with hopefulness, plunged her hands into her pockets, and she jumped for joy inside because her fingers didn't touch the bottom of the pockets, but instead sunk into two little heaps of salt. She curled up the ends of her fingers, grabbing a pinch of salt in each hand and then took a step towards the little boy.

"What are you doing?" Beth hissed.

Instead of replying with words, Evie leapt forward and rubbed one handful of salt onto the boy's face, leaving the other handful of salt for the moment when the boy opened his mouth in surprise. Then she tossed it in. He spat and coughed and Evie was hoping so hard that that little bit of salt would be enough to kill the Kratnids inside the poor little boy, but Beth didn't want to wait around to find out. She realised that whatever it had done, it had at least caused a distraction and they were then able to slip past him. So she did so, pulling Evie along with her by the arm.

They stopped halfway across the oval however, and looked back.

"I'd rather check that he's okay from back here, that's all," explained Beth. "If he's not, we can get more salt to him later."

"Fine by me," said Evie, and they stood for a short while on the oval catching their breath.

The next time they looked up, they were surrounded. The other children, having nothing to do now that the water supply had been turned off, had gathered. They moved, like zombies, closer and closer to the girls. They had already missed their chance to run. No more salt in sight. Beth's attempts at talking her students back into their old selves failed . . . In other words, they were in desperate need of some help.

While Paulo was forced to have more and more faith in the thickness and durability of his spacesuit as he encountered monster after growing monster, the Captain was busy seeing Ruby safely to another part of the gym building—a dry part. After being satisfied with a spot underneath the desk of one of the offices, he hurried back into the pool room, not intending for one minute to leave poor Paulo in there alone with them for too long. However, his job now was not to rescue Paulo, but to head straight to the drain line of the swimming pool and hook up the hose the way Beth had done earlier to drain the water out. His plan worked perfectly in theory. But in this next moment, the theory was going to have to be put to the test. It was in this same moment, that many lives, possibly even the whole world would either be saved, or doomed. Because the Captain had no plan B.

He plugged one end of the hose into the drain line of the pool, quickly found the other end and picked it up. Aiming it high above the tall, scraggly, grey, hairy Kratnids surrounding—almost smothering Paulo, he turned on the flow and water from the swimming pool came rushing through the rubber coils and the hose bulged with the discoloured, salty water. And when it came bursting out of the end in the Captain's hand (his thumb placed half way across the hole to create a wider spray), it was like a sudden downpour of rain, absolutely drenching Paulo and the already-wet Kratnids.

At first, things were not looking good. The Kratnids were not detained at all. In fact, they acted as though things were getting better for them, and the Captain suddenly knew that the water wasn't salty enough. To the Kratnids, it just seemed like more water—all the better for growing. All the better for spreading.

Paulo could see teeth in front of him. Much bigger Kratnid teeth than they had seen in that little container in the Train. The hair on their faces all mangled up with them, and their eyes a glowing yellow. A long hairy arm loomed down on Paulo, grabbing his helmet with the span of its hand and Paulo could tell that it intended on crushing him with one easy squeeze. But something made it stop. Its arm seized up and started shaking wildly as if it was being burned by a terrible acid. Paulo looked around and found that the same thing was happening to all the other Kratnids around him. They not only stopped attacking him, but they also started to pay all their attention on themselves—looking at their skin and grabbing different parts of their bodies with their hands as though every part of them was screaming out in pain.

Paulo saw his opportunity and jumped out of the corner he had been driven into, ran to the Captain's side and watched from there.

He'd finally seen the fullness of the Captain's plan, from beginning to end, and he shook his head in admiration.

"It's working!" he cried, with a smile from ear to ear. "It's working!!"

The Captain, as though watering the garden or simply spraying your common-old-garden pest with insecticide on a Sunday afternoon, was squirting the pool water all over the large Kratnids, the small Kratnids, and the medium-sized Kratnids, and then walked all around the room, soaking every part of the walls, floor and ceiling, making sure that every single microscopic Kratnid was getting a dose.

He and Paulo watched the Kratnids with mixed emotions, as their bodies started to give up and slowly topple to the ground, one by one. They became weaker and weaker and the noises they made as they fell down in pain were very difficult to listen to. Paulo's heart was both jumping for joy and crying with pity. But he knew there just wasn't any other way.

Afterwards, there was plenty of water left in the pool, so the Captain was going to do a proper job. He raced outside, dragging the hose with him and ran around the school yard like a mad man spraying anti-pest solution all over everywhere. Of course, the oval was where he came to next, and the six children surrounding Evie and Beth (including the little boy who had recently been cured), all got soaked and soon, the Kratnids inside them died away and left perfectly healthy little human bodies behind.

Beth saw to each of the children immediately to check they were okay, while the Captain kept running around in his spacesuit, spraying salty water everywhere. Beth felt a spray of water cover her lightly and she straightened up and gave the Captain a fierce look. He called back, "Sorry!", but this was not enough. Beth marched over to him, grabbed the hose from him and sprayed him until his spacesuit was completely drenched. Evie looked up and saw what was happening and laughed. She was the first. Then Paulo broke out into laughter as well and yelled out, "He's bone dry in there!"

So Evie snuck up behind the Captain and ripped off his helmet. Straight away, he got a face full of mucky, salty water. He closed his eyes and took it, pausing there a while, before he lunged out suddenly, grabbed the hose and turned it on Evie.

She squealed and jumped back, opening her mouth in shock, only to wind up with a mouthful of salty water and the odd piece of soggy potato chip, and she tried to steal the hose off the Captain.

Beth was laughing and Paulo ran over and stripped the Captain of his spacesuit. Evie laughed and laughed to see the Captain try to grab the hose off her again. Beth tried to help Evie.

"Oh!" shouted Paulo. "Boys onto girls is it?"

"Absolutely!" Beth said, taking Paulo's helmet off.

The Captain looked at Paulo, still protected in his spacesuit, and so he tore it off leaving Paulo in his sky blue overalls, getting soaked like the rest of them.

The hose got snatched out of the Captain's hand again at one stage and it flopped down onto the wet grass, and there was a fifth person who picked it up and sprayed the lot of them all at once. It was Ruby, who had found her way out of the gym building and wanted to join in the fun. The other seven children joined Ruby and suddenly, it was children against grown-ups.*

Evie stole the hose off the children again and sprayed them all and they screamed and squealed and laughed until their tummies hurt.

Then the Captain stole it once more and decided to spin around and around really fast, so it would create a rapid-fire of water that would be impossible to dodge . . . and the next thing everybody heard was . . .

"Do you have any more orders for me, Mr. Captain?"

The Captain stopped and right there amongst them was the Questing Android, still in his 'detective' hat and long coat but with a mechanical face. Then, there was a spark in his face and a little curl of smoke rising from it, before he keeled over and collapsed onto the lawn.

"You've killed him!" cried Evie, scared that poor Mr. John Quest had walked his last mechanical step and spoken his last fake-human sentence.

"He's just short circuited," said the Captain, throwing the hose down and bending over to examine the android. This put an end to the fun and games. "Miss Reynolds, you can turn off the tap for now. I'll check the whole place over with my Miniature Portable Microscope later and do some more hosing down if necessary. And er . . . you might want to take these children home and explain everything to them."

---

* If you can call any of them grown-ups at this point.

"That's not going to be easy," Beth said, and then headed off to stop the water flowing through the hose.

"So, that's it then?" said Evie next, short of breath. "No more Kratnids? That's done it? A big crazy water fight saved the world?"

"Pretty much. We've got a lot of cleaning up to do now though.

"What were you doing here in the first place, Ruby?" asked one of the little boys all of a sudden. "Do you sleep here at night?"

"We knew you were a teacher's pet, but we didn't know you were that much," put in another one.

"Yeah, that's just weird. But it's because you don't have a mum or dad. You haven't got a proper home, so you have to sleep at school." It was the one with the lisp again.

Then both of them chanted, "Teacher's pet, teacher's pet, teacher's pet, teacher's pet . . ."

Evie was looking at Ruby and saw a tiny little bead of water dropping out of the corner of her eye.

She could take no more. "Do you guys *know* what Ruby's been through?"

They stopped their chanting and looked up at Evie, unsure of how to react to her.

"She's had to deal with not having her parents around all the time, she's had to come and live in a different country from where she was born, get used to living with her grandmother, make all new friends, fight for her life against the invasion of the Kratnids from another planet, and worst of all, she's had to put up with being teased and called names by you guys!! What's so horrible about her that makes her deserve that? What has she ever done to you? Huh? And what makes you so perfect that you think you can judge others? I could pick on those front teeth of yours that haven't grown back yet, or those freckles on your nose and cheeks, or the fact that you can't sing for peanuts! But it wouldn't get me anywhere in life. And it certainly wouldn't help me in getting more friends! So stop picking on Ruby and start thinking about what faults you might have, inside. And how you might be able to fix them. Ruby can't help who she is or what circumstances she's in. Not that there's anything wrong with anything about her in the first place. She's a beautiful little girl that God made just like He made you. And the last thing He'd want to see is someone picking on His own creation. What if you made something and you were really proud of it and someone said it looked funny or it didn't work properly? How would you feel? Huh?"

The Captain had come up behind her and he now put an arm around her shoulder. Evie hadn't noticed it but while she had been talking, a few tears had escaped her own eyes.

While she took another breath to say some more, the Captain said gently to her, "That'll do."

She took a huge breath and let it all out in a short huff.

The Captain said gently, "Would I be right in thinking . . . that those were *your* bullies for a moment there? You know. From the past."

Evie shrugged sulkily. She wasn't sure whether she wanted anybody to know that she was bullied for no particular reason back in junior school.

The Captain smiled tenderly and patted her on the shoulder, before moving away again.

The boys around Ruby said no more. And soon, Beth was back from her first job, so the subject quickly changed.

"Alright, boys and girls. I'm going to get you dried up a bit and then I'm going to take you all back home so you can go back to bed! I'll explain everything that just happened on the way, how does that sound? And before you start, Samuel and Justin, I need you to know that Ruby's had a very hard few days so you need to respect that and treat her the way you would like to be treated."

The two boys she had spoken to were the ones who had been teasing Ruby. She'd expected them to say something nasty. They were renowned in the playground for teasing and name-calling.

What Beth didn't expect was the reply that came from the one with the lisp. "We weren't going to say anything else, Miss Reynolds."

". . . Oh, well . . . good. Remember that passage we learnt in the Bible the other day about making sure what we say only encourages people and doesn't put them down."

They mumbled something in agreement and merged in with the other children, in a group behind the teacher.

Beth looked up and her eyes met the Captain's. "Well, I should take these babies home. I'll probably have to explain to a few parents as well. And I suppose I'll explain everything to the school too. Shooting star, it's much easier leaving with you than staying behind, being left with all the explaining to do." Beth looked tired all of a sudden. "Well, if I don't see you before you . . . take off again . . . goodbye. And it was lovely meeting you. Well, lovely to have been met by you . . . if you know what I mean."

"I've got a lot of questions for you," he said.

"Now's not the time. Don't worry. We'll meet again. Well, for you at least. Don't know about me. But I hope so."

Before the Captain could say anything else, Beth was saying goodbye to Evie and Paulo.

"We made a great team didn't we?" she said to Evie. "It was a pleasure making salty soup with you and being in stitches from laughing so hard."

Evie agreed and smiled her big, child-like smile.

Beth hugged her, then hugged Paulo as well and then took off with the children, saying, "Full steam ahead, kiddos! Car park ahoy!"

"So, let me get this straight," said Evie, as the three of them were carrying the Questing Android back to the Train with them. "The Omrans wanted to get rid of the Kratnids themselves, because they were being a deadly pest on their planet too?"

"Ah-huh."

"But their ship went out of control, so they went off course and crash-landed right here in Eternal Promise Christian School."

"Yep."

"All in a day's work for you, isn't it, Captain?"

"Quite. Nearly there," he said as they were approaching the Train. He was the only one who knew they were approaching the Train of course, because he was wearing his glasses with the special lenses in them that enabled him to see his beautiful steam-engine spaceship.

He got the key out of his pocket and they carefully walked in with the android. The Captain laid the android down on the floor of the engine room and opened up his chest—where the works were.

"Oh! This is easily fixed," he said to himself and then got to work.

"What are you going to do once you've fixed him?" asked Evie.

He didn't answer immediately. Evie and Paulo were patient enough to wait until he'd finished the repair work, and then watched him fossicking around in a deep drawer that was a part of the control deck at the very front of the Train.

"I'm going to use this!" he said triumphantly, pulling out a small object that looked just like his Atom Relocating Molecular Teleport Device.*

"Captain," said Paulo. "That's your Atom Relocating Molecular Teleport Device!"

"Correction, *this* is my Atom Relocating Molecular Teleport Device." He whipped out the one from his pocket. "*This* one," he said, wiggling the one he'd taken out of the drawer, "is another one I built a long time ago. Got buried down here and I forgot all about it. Now it'll come in handy." He got to work, attaching the thing to the android. "I'm going to send him back to Omrah, (I know the coordinates from looking at the flight deck of the Omran space ship earlier), and give him a message to send to them . . . Except not in that order." He activated

---

* A device he always kept in one of his pockets. Press a button and you could be somewhere else in seconds. But once used, it took twenty-four hours to charge up fully again for the next use. So it had to be used wisely.

the Questing Android and spoke to it. "John, me old pal. Are you back with us?"

"All systems go. How do you do, Mr. Captain? Great weather for the time of year wouldn't you say?"

"Yes, but never mind that now. I'm sending you back to Omrah and you're to give your creators or commanders or whoever sent you on your mission, this message . . . Now let me see, you already know about the crash-landing . . . 'The Kratnids that escaped the ship as a result of the crash have been dealt with. So . . . Mission Accomplished, really. But the Earth people send their condolences for the two who risked their lives for that mission.'" The Captain thought for a bit, and then said, "That'll do."

"Affirmative. Lovely to meet you, Mr. Captain and company."

They all smiled and said farewell before the Captain ordered the android to press the button on the Atom Relocating Molecular Teleport Device. There was a funny tingling in the air, and he disappeared.

"I've never sent an intergalactic telegram before," said the Captain.

"Is that what it was?" asked Paulo, eagerly.

"I guess. I just made that up then. Rather '*cool*' as you might say."

It was then that they noticed the dead Kratnid in the glass container sitting on the central control deck—above where the furnace was.

"We'd better dispose of this," said the Captain.

"It's amazing how something as simple as salt was the answer," Evie reflected.

"We have Sodium Chloride on Serothia too," said Paulo.

"It makes sense when you look back. They relied on water to survive, salt dries it up. But it was more than that—their bodies obviously had an intolerance to salt."

There was a long silence after that as they reflected on everything. The Captain was genuinely reflecting, but Evie and Paulo's faces had changed. They wanted to know about a certain Beth Reynolds. They pictured her in their minds . . . kissing the Captain!

Reading their smirking expressions, the Captain burst out, saying, "I don't know her from a bar of soap! I know of no reason whatsoever why that woman would do such a thing. Anyway, she'd been taken over by the Kratnids and they wanted to take over me, so in fact, there was a very good reason!"

"She knows you well though."

The Captain shrugged. "I'm a traveller. Happens all the time. It's nothing surprising. Shall we go? Your mum and dad will be worried sick about you, Evelyn. Perhaps we should go back in time so that you've only been gone a minute."

"Taking the rubbish out."

"Pardon?"

"I was taking the rubbish out. Before Beth kidnapped me."

"Right, well I'll land the Train just near the bins then. A minute after you were kidnapped."

"But it's just to let them know I'm okay, right? And then I can come back on the Train with you and Paulo?"

The Captain hesitated. "I don't have a problem with that, but your parents might."

"What if you tell them it's an educational trip. Because I am learning heaps, you know, I've learnt how to turn the water off and on, what foods have lots of salt in them, especially processed foods, like cans of stuff and cereal, and I've learnt that male alligators are on average four to five metres long and the females are only about three metres long." She paused and looked at the Captain and Paulo looking back at her. "It was on a little information board thing at the zoo."*

"She's right, Captain," said Paulo suddenly. "I've learnt quite a lot too. You said you'd show me who your mysterious friend is. The . . . Ancient of Days you called Him. And a bunch of other names. And I've learnt a bit about Him because He sounded so wonderful the way you described him. You showed me a tiny baby and said that was Him. You talked about having a safe sanctuary, a place where you can rest and said *that* was Him. What have you got for me this time?"

"Okay . . ." he thought for a while. "Well I guess you could say He's a bit like salt. That powerful substance that saved our lives. And He wants us to be like salt too. What do you know about salt, Evelyn?"

"Erm . . ." suddenly, Evie felt like she was in the classroom, being put on the spot by the science teacher. "You put it on chips."

"To . . ." the Captain prompted.

"To give it more flavour, it gives flavour!"

---

* Incidentally, speaking of reptiles, the crocodile that escaped the Adelaide Zoo at the opening of this story was recaptured within another day with hardly any hassles (apart from an unfortunate young zoo keeper who had to cancel his first date he'd spent so much time plucking up the courage to make, with an attractive young lady called Sophie.) And you'll be happy to know that no people or crocodiles were harmed during the process.

"And?"

"Um . . . it's used as a preservative. And it stings when you put it on a cut. But it's good for it apparently."

"And . . . it's very drying," added Paulo.

"Which means . . ." he asked Evie.

"Well . . . that . . . if you eat lots, you get thirsty. It makes you thirsty."

"Yes."

"So . . ." Paulo was confused. "Your friend . . . what's-his-name?"

"Jesus."

"Makes you thirsty."

"In one sense, yes." He looked at Paulo with a mysterious, enticing grin. "Aren't you thirsty?"

Paulo didn't answer with words but with a small smile back. He knew the answer must have been yes, otherwise he wouldn't be asking all these questions and he wouldn't have bothered coming for a ride on the Train in the first place.

"Anyway," said the Captain, starting up the big steam engine with a *chuff chooety chuff choofety chuff choofety bang!* As he got to work, he looked up at a little scrap piece of paper that looked like it was blue-tacked to a bit of blank wall in the engine room, near the front window. The words **salt and light** were plainly hand-written in blue ink and he stared at the words meaningfully. Those two short words were many things to the Captain. His past, his present and his future. A reminder of why he was alive. Why he'd been *allowed* to live. And every time he saw those words, he made a promise—to himself, and to the Great One.

Chapter Nineteen

Home Time

It was a sunny day. Gentle breeze blowing, cheerful birds singing, steam engine chuffing. The Captain had landed the Train in the Bamfords' backyard successfully. It was the middle of the day. They walked out boldly, Evie all prepared to close the lid of that bin and then run back inside to see mum. This time, setting aside the time to explain everything to her *and* dad properly.

As soon as they stepped out of the carriage though, they saw that something was terribly wrong. Police cars were lining the street. Policemen and women were everywhere—striding around her backyard like they owned the place—talking on their walky-talkies and listening to the muffled replies from the station. Evie's stomach churned as worry for her family grew quickly inside her. She ran up to one of the policemen and demanded, "What's going on? What's happened? I don't get it, I've only been gone a minute. How did you all get here so soon?"

Paulo and the Captain came up behind her.

The policeman in front of Evie frowned, but then his eyes widened and his jaw dropped. He hurriedly took a photograph out of his pocket, looked back at Evie's face and then got on his walky-talky. "We've found her. Call off the search party. She's safe and sound by the looks."

"Evelyn?" came a desperate voice from inside the house and out came running Evie's mum. Her hair unfussy, dark circles round her eyes, tear-stained cheeks. "Evie!!!"

Evie was almost knocked over by her mum's embrace.

"What? What's happened?"

"Where have you been?" She let go to look at her daughter. "With these two men again?" Then she spoke to Paulo and the Captain. "Who are you? What do you want with my daughter?"

"Captain, did you get the time right?" Paulo whispered.

"Mum, I've been at Eternal Promise Christian School. Only for the night, but it's supposed to be that same day . . . isn't it?" She looked questioningly at the Captain.

He answered out the corner of his mouth. "Ah . . . no guarantee. I keep forgetting about the repairs I still have to make on the navigation system that Mallory messed up."

"You've been gone for *days*," Madeline Bamford cried.

Evie and the crew of the Train gasped.

James and Paul Bamford soon came running outside too, as soon as they heard Evie's voice. There was a touching reunion, and the Captain found it all very awkward.

The natural progression of things brought Evie and her family inside, yet she was busting to show them the Train.

While the Captain and Paulo waited patiently inside the Train, Evie and James were just finishing explaining everything. Right from the moment Evie first met the Captain and the whole story of Satellite SB-17 where they first met Paulo.

They somehow knew the stories must be true because both of their children were telling them. It was especially more credible as soon as James vouched for all the tales. He was not usually one to waste time telling jokes and pulling pranks.

"Well you don't actually have to take our word for it," said Evie. "I want to show you the Train itself! Come on!"

"Yeah, let's go!" said James, excited at the thought of getting a tour of the old steam locomotive that had been converted into a space and time machine. He'd seen inside it of course, when he and Lisa were taken home from the zoo, but he ran like a little boy after Evie, out to the backyard to see it again and get a proper tour.

"Will you do a quick tour for my mum and dad?" Evie said as she and her brother burst in through the carriage door.

"Well, alright but where are they?"

"They're still not sure about everything," said James. "They're just a bit slow. I'll go get them." He disappeared again and ran across the backyard to hurry them along.

"Have you suggested to them that you would rather not stop travelling yet?" the Captain asked Evie in the quiet Train carriage. Him and Paulo were seated on one of the comfy sofas, and as Evie answered, she sat herself on the other one opposite.

"No, not yet. I thought they might be more likely to say yes if they had the tour of the Train first."

Just then, it suddenly got a little dimmer in the carriage room. The sun pouring in from the open door had been blocked, for somebody was standing there. It wasn't James. And it was neither of the Bamford parents.

When they recognised who it was, they stood up, and gave the woman a warm smile.

"Beth?" said Evie.

"Miss Reynolds?" said the Captain, surprised.

"What are you doing here? I thought we said goodbye at the school." Evie was happy to see her.

Beth had a strange bland expression on her face, standing there stiffly in the doorway. But then, quickly she smiled and said, "I've got something to show you."

With that, she stepped right inside the Train, walked past them all and headed straight to the engine room. The Captain, naturally, was the first to follow her, frowning in confusion.

As the Captain entered, Beth was pressing buttons on the central control deck.

"What are you doing? Hey, that's the navigation system."

"I know. It's in a terrible state." She kept pressing buttons and started operating lots of different controls around the whole room.

"Miss Reynolds, do you know what you're doing?"

"Of course I do."

"It looks to me like you're trying to set coordinates."

"Then you would be correct."

"Beth, we can't go anywhere, my parents are on their way. I've got to tell them, *ask* them something important."

"*This* is important." She did not look up from her work.

The Captain couldn't let her continue, for two reasons. One: He wasn't about to be responsible for kidnapping the Bamfords' daughter a third time without having their permission.* And two: he had only really just met this woman and so could not allow himself to trust her so easily.

The Captain stepped forward and tried to stop Beth from whatever she was doing, but as he did so, the Train's outer door slammed shut with a heavy *thud* and the engine fired up and grew louder and louder as more and more steam built up.

"I think we're taking off, Captain," said Paulo. "Are you going to do something?"

"Just trust me, can't you?" said Beth calmly. "You've got no other choice."

It fell silent in the Train, (apart from the engine noise) because the three travellers were quite speechless, looking on with worried and baffled curiosity. And because of this silence, they could hear the tune that Beth was humming to herself as she drove the Train rapidly, but calmly, into space. It was a tune they had heard in the playground not long ago. A tune with words that were growing strangely familiar to them.

The tune and the words had become a mystery. Even though it was as simple as a harmless children's song:

We're following the leader, the leader, the leader,
We're following the leader, wherever he may go . . .

---

* I am sure of whether 'kidnap' is the right word if you *do* have the care-takers' permission, but anyway.

On that day, at that very hour, in that precise minute, at Eternal Promise Christian School, the real Beth Reynolds sat down with her class and told them about the wombat. She explained that there were no more potentially unfriendly furry friends around because of a very good friend of hers who thought up a brilliant plan to get rid of them. In Art that day, they all made 'thank you' cards to Captain Johns, Evie and Paulo who helped Miss Reynolds save the school. And while their little hands were busy colouring, cutting, gluing and writing, Beth wondered when she would see her good friend, the Captain again.

*   *   *

"Salt is good, but if it loses its saltiness, how can you make it salty again? Have salt in yourselves, and be at peace with each other."—Mark 9:50

"Don't go to bed angry, don't steal anymore, watch the way you talk. Let nothing foul or dirty come out of your mouth. Don't give the Devil these kinds of footholds in your life. Say only what helps and builds others up according to their needs—that it may benefit those who listen. Each word a gift."—From Ephesians 4:27-29

"Everything we know about God's Word is summed up in a single sentence: love others as you love yourself. If you keep on biting and devouring each other, watch out or you will be destroyed by each other."—Galatians 5:14-15

"As the deer pants for streams of water, so my soul pants for you, my God. My soul thirsts for God, for the living God."—Psalm 42:1-2

"Come, all you who are thirsty; come to the waters."—Isaiah 55:1

"Furry Friends" Facts

The Universe

The 'Tuba' Galaxy is another made up name. There has been no such name given to a galaxy that I am aware of.

The World Around Us

Everything the Captain said about living organism classification is, to the best of my knowledge, true. Most of this knowledge, I credit to my year eleven biology teacher—and the way he made it so interesting. Thanks Mr K!

The Adelaide Zoo at the time of writing this doesn't have crocodiles, but they do have alligators.

One way to tell a crocodile from an alligator is by looking at their mouths. An alligator's mouth is long and pointy, whereas the crocodile's mouth is shorter and much more rounded. They also have teeth that are visible from the outside when their mouth is closed, whereas the alligator's teeth are not visible unless he or she is yawning, about to catch some food, or doing an impersonation of a crocodile in the only way he or she knows how. ♣

Around about 70% of the Earth is covered in water. And it varies within different people, but on average, 60% of the human body is made up of water. 70% of your brain is made up of water and wait for it . . . 90% of your lungs is water!

♣   Sorry, that last little bit probably isn't a fact and so never should have made it onto this page.

The Captain's 'Beatles' Quotes

"Slow down baby, now you're movin' way too fast."
    from the song "Slow Down"

"I have always thought that it's a crime. So I will ask you once
    again."
        from the song "We Can Work It Out"

"We can work it out and get it straight or say goodnight."
    from the song "We Can Work It Out"

(Evie's Beatles Quote:) "Getting better all the time."
    from the song "Getting Better"